Evangeline Mudd

and the GREAT Mink Escapade

Evangeline Mudd

and the
GREAT
Mink
Escapade

DAVID ELLIOTT

ILLUSTRATED BY
ANDRÉA WESSON

CANDLEWICK PRESS
CAMBRIDGE, MASSACHUSETTS

Text copyright © 2006 by David Elliott
Illustrations copyright © 2006 by Andréa Wesson

First edition 2006

Library of Congress Cataloging-in-Publication Data

Elliott, David, date.
Evangeline Mudd and the great mink escapade / David Elliott ;
illustrated by Andréa Wesson. — 1st ed.
p. cm.
Summary: Keeping a promise to her friends in
the Pals United for Furry Friends organization, ten-year-old
Evangeline returns to Mudd Manor to try to rescue a group
of minks before they are turned into ballet costumes.
ISBN-10 0-7636-2295-8
ISBN-13 978-0-7636-2295-4
[1. Minks—Fiction. 2. Ballet dancing—Fiction.
3. Humorous stories.] I. Title: Great mink escapade.
II. Wesson, Andréa, ill. III. Title.

PZ7.E447Evg 2006
[Fic]—dc22   2005054260

2 4 6 8 10 9 7 5 3 1

Printed in the United States of America

This book was typeset in Plantin.

Candlewick Press
2067 Massachusetts Avenue
Cambridge, Massachusetts 02140

visit us at www.candlewick.com

To Ulrike Sawicki, the real Rick

Chapter 1

URGENT!!!

I wonder if you can imagine how Evangeline Mudd felt on the day this story begins. After all, not so long ago, she had been whisked through a jungle in the arms of a four-hundred-pound ape. She'd rubbed noses with a headhunter. Why, she had even broken the Law of the Jungle. But now all that was over. Now she was home, safe and sound with her parents at their cozy bungalow in New England.

It wouldn't be fair to say that Evangeline was unhappy. After all, she had spent most of her time away wishing that she *could be* home. It's just that, well, now she had a great deal in common with those kids in countries where parents give them slices of pineapple sprinkled in red-hot chili pepper.

The first time those kids have that snack, their eyes practically bug out of their heads. Their faces turn pink, then maroon, and then a lovely shade of vermilion. Tears stream from their eyes. "Call a doctor!" they holler as they run in circles, looking for buckets of water to dunk their heads in. "Call the police! Call the fire department!"

But then, after the hullabaloo has died down and the pineapple is gone, and the kids are back to normal, the strangest thing happens. "Please," the kids say to their parents, "give us more."

Yes, Evangeline was very much like those children. In other words, she had had one adventure, and she was dying to have another.

On the afternoon in question, the sunlight was filtering through the canopy of the trees, dappling the leaves in a way that made them seem like the feathers of a fantastic bird. Evangeline was brachiating, hand over hand, in a stand of maples that grew behind the cozy bungalow. (Brachiating, by the way, is how monkeys and apes get around in this world—by swinging from one branch to another. Evangeline was an expert brachiator.)

This is terrific, she thought as she reached for a branch just over her head. *But it would be so much better if I were being chased by a gorilla.*

She was just about to do a double flip when she
heard her mother calling from below.

Magdalena's voice was such that no matter how
loudly she spoke, she seemed to be reciting the sweetest
poetry. This was especially true when she was speaking
to Evangeline.

"Perhaps you'd better come down now, dear. The
mail has just arrived. There's a letter for you."

A letter! Evangeline landed on the next limb with
both feet. Hugging the maple's smooth trunk as if it
were a long-lost friend, she scrambled her way to the
ground.

The letter could be from only one person. Dr.
Aphrodite Pikkaflee, the world's most famous

primatologist and the very person with whom Evangeline had had her adventure in the jungle! Dr. Pikkaflee had already written Evangeline several letters telling her of the progress she was making with the jungle school she had started.

Evangeline opened her arms as wide as she could and ran to her mother. Her intention, naturally, was to hug the woman. But this wasn't as easy as you might think. At present, Magdalena was as round as a beach ball. Evangeline would have a brother or sister very soon.

"Where's the letter from Dr. Pikkaflee?" Evangeline asked, her arms encircling what they could of her mother's generous middle.

"It's on the kitchen table, darling. Right next to the gooseberry jam." Magdalena picked at her daughter's scalp exactly the way a golden-haired ape mother might do.

Evangeline let go of Magdalena and ran toward the house.

"But the letter isn't from Dr. Pikkaflee, dear," her mother called out.

Evangeline stopped in her tracks. If it wasn't from Dr. Aphrodite Pikkaflee, then who could it be from? Evangeline wasn't the kind of girl who got a lot of letters. After all, she was only ten years old.

She turned back to her mother, who had plunked herself down in the grass at the base of the trees. "The return address says Eversharp," Magdalena said. A hummingbird flew around her head, momentarily mistaking her reddish curls for a bouquet of snapdragons. "Miss B. Eversharp."

Evangeline wracked her brain.

"But I've never heard of someone named B. Eversharp," she said at last.

"Are you sure?" her mother asked, smiling at the hummingbird. "She certainly seems to have heard of you, because on the back of the letter, B. Eversharp has written URGENT in big black letters and has punctuated it with three exclamation points."

At this, the hummingbird zoomed up into the trees.

Now, if you ever get a letter from a stranger marked URGENT, your heart should start to speed up a bit because URGENT usually means one of two things. One: You owe someone a great deal of money, and she wants you to pay it back as soon as possible.

As far as she knew, Evangeline didn't owe any money, except five cents to the local library for a book she had returned one day late. She couldn't imagine that the librarian would send her a letter with URGENT written on the back, and certainly not URGENT followed by three exclamation points. Besides, the librarian's name was Emanuel Bopp, not Miss B. Eversharp.

That meant that this was the second kind of URGENT, the kind where someone is in terrible trouble and needs help. And naturally, if that kind of urgent is written in big black letters and is followed by not one but *three* exclamation points, well, then, it probably means that you must take action immediately.

Evangeline turned toward the house and ran as if she *were* being chased by a gorilla, for *action* is a word that is very closely related to another, and that word, of course, is *adventure*.

Chapter 2

Near the Meadow of the Beavers

When Evangeline reached the kitchen, she found her father sitting at the breakfast table. In his left hand, he was twirling a pencil. In his right hand, he balanced a pad of paper. He seemed to be making some kind of list.

"Hello, Merry," she said. "What's up?"

The tall man's name was Merriweather. Sometimes Evangeline called him Father, but other days she addressed him as Merry. This was definitely a Merry day. He had a faraway look in his eyes and was smiling a faraway, dreamy kind of smile.

"Hello, dear," he said, blinking behind his glasses. "I was wondering if you could help me."

Evangeline wanted to get to that letter, but her father was very dear to her. When he asked for her help, there was nothing she could do but give it.

"I've been trying to think of names for your new brother or sister," he said. "What do you think of *Bud*?"

"Bud Mudd?" Evangeline asked. "Too rhymey."

"Ah yes," her father answered, crossing *Bud* off the list. "Too rhymey. I suppose *Judd* has the same problem?"

"I'm afraid so," Evangeline replied.

She could see the letter propped against the gooseberry jam. With no effort at all, she could merely reach out and take it.

"How about *Fabiano*?" her father asked. "It means bean farmer, you know."

It struck Evangeline instantly that she did not want a brother named Bean Farmer, not that she had anything against beans. Or farmers either, for that matter. But when she imagined having a brother named Bean Farmer, a vague sense of disaster seemed to pass through her.

"What about girls' names?" she asked.

He flipped a page on his pad of paper.

"So far I have three: *Pamelia, Beverly,* and *Bikita.*"

"*Pamelia*'s nice," Evangeline said, hoping to hurry things along. "What does *it* mean?"

"Covered with honey," her father replied enthu-
siastically.

Merriweather was the kind of father who was
enthusiastic about practically everything.

"How about *Beverly*, then?" she said.

"Beverly," her father replied. "Near the meadow of
the beavers."

"What was that *third* name?" Evangeline asked.

"Bikita," Merriweather replied. "It's African."

"Bikita," Evangeline repeated. There was something about the name she liked. *B* and *K* and *T* were such strong letters, strong letters for a strong sister. "Bikita Mudd. I *like* it."

"I'm glad, darling, because I do too. Unfortunately, Magdalena objects. You know that I love your mother, Evangeline dear, but the plain truth is she *can* be rather stubborn."

Evangeline had never known her mother to be stubborn. In fact, when she objected to a thing, which was exceedingly rare, there was almost always a good reason for it.

"Excuse me, Merry," the girl said, "but what exactly does *Bikita* mean?"

Her father brushed a crumb from the table, turning his gaze to the window as he did so.

"Anteater," he said.

"Merry?" Evangeline asked. "Could I help you with this later?"

"By all means, dear. We don't have to decide on a name today. We have plenty of time."

This was true. Besides, Evangeline knew that her mother and father would go through hundreds, possibly thousands, of names before they decided. It had taken them weeks to choose a name for their book about their adventure with the golden-haired apes of the Ikkinasti Jungle. And this was a *baby* they were naming, not just a book.

Her father stood up. As always, Evangeline was amazed that his head did not bump the ceiling.

"I think I'll go and talk to your mother about *Bikita*," he said. "There is no reason on Earth we shouldn't have a daughter named Anteater."

"Magdalena, darling," she heard him call as he walked out the door and into the garden. "I've been rethinking the name . . ."

Evangeline stared at the letter leaning against the jar of gooseberry jam. The envelope was yellow, the color of daffodils when they first pop up in the spring. A garland of violets and forget-me-nots trailed down the right side.

It certainly doesn't look like the kind of letter that would be marked URGENT, Evangeline told herself. *It looks more like an invitation to a tea party.*

She reached over and picked up the letter. The scent of lilacs

11

wafted up and into her nostrils even though the lilacs around the cozy bungalow had spent their blossoms weeks ago.

Evangeline tried to imagine a person who would send an urgent letter, an URGENT with three exclamation points no less, and still take the time to perfume the letter with the scent of lilacs.

She tore open the envelope and pulled out the letter.

Dear Miss Mudd,
Once, you made a promise to help us.
If you mean to keep your promise, the
time has come. Read the newspaper
clipping I've stapled to this letter and
you'll understand why.
  Most sincerely and urgently yours,
  B. Eversharp
  President
  Pals United for Furry Friends

"So that's it!" Evangeline shouted. "B. Eversharp is the Pencil!"

Chapter 3

Oh No! Not *Her!*

Evangeline didn't make a habit of going around saying that this person is a fork or that person is a clothespin. She actually was acquainted with someone known as the Pencil. Evangeline had met the Pencil while living at Mudd's Manor, the enormously ugly house owned by Melvin, her father's second cousin, twice removed, and his wife, India Terpsichore. (This was just before her parents disappeared in the Ikkinasti Jungle, by the way.)

Evangeline had never known the Pencil's real name. She had given her that nickname because the woman was tall and thin and always wore a yellow dress. The only thing she *did* know was that the Pencil was a member of Pals United for Furry Friends, an organization whose members marched up and down in front of Mudd's Manor, chanting and waving signs that said things like MUDD'S MINKS STINK.

Melvin hated PUFF and called its members "animal nuts." Melvin, you see, earned a great deal of money turning minks into jackets and hats and all kinds of things for rich ladies and gentlemen, and Pals United for Furry Friends, or PUFF, believed that minks had the right to live as minks like to do, running about on riverbanks and not all bunched up in cages, terrified that it was their turn to become a jacket.

Evangeline had agreed with PUFF. As far as she was concerned, Melvin's business was a horrid one, almost as horrid as her father's second cousin, twice removed, himself.

In fact, Melvin's mink ranch was not a ranch at all, at least not in the way that you or I might think of a ranch, with wide-open spaces and clear blue skies. No, Melvin's mink ranch was nothing but row after row of dirty cages, cages crammed with minks — mommy minks, daddy minks, baby minks, even second-cousin, twice-removed minks.

These minks had been born in cages. They lived in cages. Some of them even died in cages. They had never dashed about a riverbank or lined a den with grass. They had never, not once, set their four paws on the soft, brown earth or caught a fish or felt the rain on their pelts. They had never even poked their noses out of a den on a summer morning, whiskers all a-twitch, thinking, *Hmmm. What mischief can I make today?* For the truth must be told: minks *are* rather mischievous creatures.

With their sharp little claws and their pointed little teeth and their bad little tempers, minks have a reputation for being rather nasty. Any farmer will tell you that minks spend a great deal of their day trying to figure out how to raid the henhouse. And here is something funny. When the animal nuts carried signs that said MUDD'S MINKS STINK, they were more right than they knew. Minks *do* stink! After all, they are cousins to skunks, and we all know what skunks are famous for.

But, Evangeline had asked herself many, many times, *just because minks might give you a nasty bite or steal your chickens or cause you to hold your nose, is that any reason to lock them up in cages and turn them into jackets?*

Evangeline, I hope you will agree, had a point. After all, minks are only following their nature, just the way you are when you bug your brother or make a fuss at bedtime or refuse to eat your peas. (And nobody wants to turn *you* into a jacket. At least, I hope they don't.)

The Pencil's letter brought it all back to her now, and what it said was correct. Evangeline *had* promised PUFF that once she had found her parents in the Ikkinasti Jungle, she would return to Mudd's Manor and save the minks.

She plopped down in the chair where her father had been sitting.

" '. . . the time has come,' " she read again. " 'Read the newspaper clipping I've stapled to this letter and you'll understand why.' "

Evangeline folded back the letter and was immediately confronted with a newspaper photograph of a ballerina wearing a tutu that frilled out around her and gave the general impression of a nasty bug hiding in a flower.

"Oh no!" the girl shouted. "Not *her*!"

But it was her. It was her dancing up a storm.

India Terpsichore Mudd was Melvin Mudd's wife. At one time, she had been a famous ballerina and had traveled around the world whirling like a dust devil and leaping like a hyena. But that had been many years ago. Now she was well past forty, which is old enough for anybody but positively ancient when it comes to ballerinas.

The photograph portrayed a very young India Terpsichore. Her left leg was flung up in the air so high over her head that her heel was directly over her nose. Her right leg was stretched out at an impossible angle to the side, and her arms seemed to be whirling in opposite directions behind her.

Underneath the picture was a caption.

"'Prima Ballerina India Terpsichore Mudd, performing *The Dance of the Dying Dung Beetle* for His Highness the Crown Prince of Burpa Ghen,'" Evangeline read. "But why should a picture of India Terpsichore cause the Pencil to send me an urgent letter?" Evangeline asked. "I had better read the article."

BALLERINA SAYS SHE'LL DANCE AGAIN
by Josephina Hinks

The once-famous ballerina India

17

Terpsichore Mudd disclosed to the press today that she will return to the stage in a full production of *Hansel and Gretel in Kaboomistan*.

Reporters were visibly stunned when the ballerina revealed that she will dance the role of Gretel. Hansel will be played by none other than world-famous Alexy Alexy. Reported to be fabulously wealthy, Alexy is the world's highest-jumping dancer.

Melvin Mudd, husband, told reporters that all the costumes for the ballet will be made of mink: "Mink tutus! Mink leotards! Mink everything! And that includes the orchestra! I'm gonna make a mint! It'll take every last mink I own!"

The article continued, but Evangeline had read enough.

"Merriweather," she called as she headed out for the garden. "Magdalena! I've got to talk to you."

Chapter 4

Welcome Aboard!

It didn't take long for Evangeline to convince her parents to let her return to Mudd's Manor. She had made a promise, and did Magdalena and Merriweather really want to raise the kind of girl who doesn't keep her promises?

Naturally, they were very reluctant to see her leave, especially with the birth of her brother or sister coming so soon. But like all good parents, Merriweather and Magdalena understood that there are times when holding a daughter back is worse than letting her go. And so, the goodbyes at the airport were similar to the ones when Evangeline had departed for Mudd's Manor the first time, with lots of tears and kissing and nose rubbing. Except that this time there was a present.

Reaching into the pocket of his jacket, Evangeline's father produced a small rectangular package wrapped in shining gold foil and tied with ribbons, the ends of which were curled up in tiny ringlets, very much like Evangeline's own.

"You are our shining star," Merriweather said proudly.

After untying the ribbons, Evangeline carefully lifted the lid from the golden box. Inside lay a fountain pen, as tidy and solemn as a mummy.

"It's so you'll remember to write us," Magdalena said softly.

The pen was a deep, iridescent blue. It reminded Evangeline of the way the ocean had looked from the windows of *The Flying Monkey,* Dr. Aphrodite Pikkaflee's plane that had carried her to Ikkinasti.

"Try it out, darling," Merriweather said, handing her the luggage tag that the ticket attendant had given them when she checked in. "But be careful: fountain pens are as temperamental as a golden-hair who has run out of bananas."

Evangeline screwed off the cap, admiring the way the pen's silver nib glinted under the bright lights of the airport terminal. But as she pressed its point against the pale yellow cardboard, a big blob of ink, the color of rosebuds just before they open, oozed out and spread across the tag like a shadow in the late afternoon.

"Oh no!" she cried. "I ruined it."

"It just takes a little practice," Magdalena reassured her. "Practice and patience, like all things worth doing."

By the time Evangeline got to the capital *M* in *Mudd*, she was already getting the hang of it. She loved the way the shining gold point of the pen made its way across the surface of the tag. When she got the pressure just right, it almost felt as if the pen were moving by itself, like a raft on a calm sea. She loved the color of the ink too.

"It's pink so we'll know right away who the letter is from," Magdalena explained.

Evangeline finished writing her name, stuck the tag to the small bag that she was carrying, and carefully tucked the pen into the bag's side pocket. It seemed to be made especially for the pen.

She gave her parents one final hug, and then, as her flight was announced and before anyone had time to have second thoughts about her going, she walked toward the gate where her plane was waiting. As she got to the door that led to the ramp, she looked back at Merriweather and Magdalena a final time.

"Don't worry," she called out. "I'll be back before the baby is born. Nothing could keep me from that."

Now, it was very clever of Evangeline to say this, because one thing about adventures, perhaps the *scariest* thing about adventures, is that it's impossible to predict how long they are going to take. (If you can, then they probably aren't adventures worth taking in the first place.)

Some adventures last for years, others for a lifetime! But the thing is, if you knew that, you would never start out on an adventure at all. That's why it's always a good idea, just before you leave, to say, "I'll be back before this or that happens"—even if you're not quite sure that you believe it. It makes everyone feel better, including the adventurer.

As Evangeline walked down the ramp, she had many things to consider. Naturally, she thought about her parents and how she would miss them. But she was not the kind of girl to dwell on such things. Before she had reached the door to the plane, her mind had turned to the problem of saving the minks.

The first thing I have to do, she thought, *is to find*

where Melvin keeps them. How can I rescue the minks if I don't know where they are?

This was a very sensible way to begin, especially since she knew that the location of the mink ranch was *top secret*. Even the rich ladies and gentlemen for whom Melvin turned minks into jackets didn't know the whereabouts of Mudd's Marvelous Minks.

Maybe I'll have to follow Melvin, like a detective, she thought. This idea appealed to the girl, and for a moment she imagined herself wearing a strange hat with a bill in the front and the back, carrying an enormous magnifying glass. But when she stepped off the ramp and into the plane, her imaginings were abruptly halted by a burly flight attendant whose name Evangeline had just enough time to read from the silver wings pinned to his massive chest. RICK, it said in square black letters.

Evangeline was expecting Rick to smile and say "Welcome aboard!" the way flight attendants are supposed to do, even if they don't mean it. Instead, Rick glowered at her as if she had just stomped on his foot.

Maybe I have *stepped on his foot,* Evangeline thought. *It's easy to do when you're on a plane.*

She was just about to say "Excuse me," just in case, when Rick snatched the boarding pass out of her hand faster than a hungry frog snatches a dragonfly off a lily pad. After inspecting the piece of paper as if it were a highly classified document, he looked up at Evangeline and squinted. Finally, he pointed to an aisle seat not far from where they stood.

"Buckle your seat belt and shut your trap!" he snarled.

Evangeline very much wanted to respond to this rudeness, but the umbrella of the gentleman behind her was poking her in the back, and so she satisfied herself by snatching her boarding pass out of Rick's hand in exactly the way he had done to her. Before Rick could say another word, she turned and made her way toward the seat he had indicated.

Being ordered about by someone in a uniform did not seem like an especially good beginning to her trip.

I'd better be prepared for anything, Evangeline decided as she walked down the narrow aisle, taking special care not to bump other passengers with her bag.

As it turned out, this was a very wise decision.

Chapter 5

Somewhere Between
Liddie and *Elsbetta*

Like Evangeline, the girl in the seat next to hers seemed to be traveling alone. She was a pale girl, with dirty blond hair that she had attempted to pull back into a ponytail but that looked much more like the tail of a large mouse, especially since this hairstyle exposed the girl's tremendous ears.

"My name is Libby. Libby Heck," the pale girl said.

"My name is Evangeli—"

"It's a nickname for *Elizabeth. Libby,* I mean," blurted the girl.

Evangeline considered it very impolite of Libby to have interrupted her like that, but later, as the plane was lifting off from the runway, a wave of sympathy began to rise for the girl.

Maybe she's just nervous, Evangeline decided. *Maybe she doesn't like being in airplanes, or maybe this is the first time she is away from her parents.*

After all, it had not been so long ago when she, Evangeline herself, had been separated from her parents for the first time. She could remember clearly how frightening it felt.

Once the plane had reached its cruising altitude, Evangeline tried again.

"My name is Evangeli—" she began.

"*Betsy* is another nickname for *Elizabeth,*" Libby Heck broke in, taking a sip of the watered-down orange juice that Rick had slammed in front of her. "You probably didn't know that."

Libby Heck, Evangeline soon discovered, was positively stuck on nicknames—nicknames for *Elizabeth,* that is. She wasn't the slightest bit interested in Evangeline or where Evangeline might be going or for what reason. She was interested only in herself and the various choices she could call herself.

Hundreds of miles later, Evangeline hadn't completed a single sentence. She had given up somewhere between *Liddie* and *Elsbetta.* But that wasn't the worst thing. The worst thing was that Libby Heck had prattled on so that Evangeline hadn't been able to give any thought to how she was going to find the minks or how she was going to explain to her father's second cousin, twice removed, and his wife that she was back at Mudd's Manor.

When she had left with Aphrodite Pikkaflee, she had closed the door behind her without a single word. Just a simple note that said, "I'm leaving."

Maybe, thought Evangeline, in the one minute that Libby Heck had gone to beg Rick for peanuts, *maybe I'll do the same thing. But this time I'll just say, "I'm here."*

Finally, the plane began to makes its long, unhurried descent.

"I tried *Lilibeth* for a week," Libby Heck shouted over the roar of the engines.

The last thing Libby said to her was, "You should change your name to *Elizabeth. Evangeli?* What a silly name!"

They were standing at the baggage carousel. Out of the corner of her eye, Evangeline saw Rick stomp by, swinging his small bag like a hammer.

Not long after, Evangeline found herself walking up the sidewalk that led to Mudd's Manor. She still hadn't the slightest idea of how she was going to explain her presence there. Not only that, but PUFF was nowhere to be seen.

This filled the girl with a sense of foreboding. In

the three months she had spent at the horrible house before her adventure in the Ikkinasti Jungle, B. Eversharp and her friends had never missed a day making a racket in front of Mudd's Manor. Without them, the house seemed like an enormous cuckoo clock whose cuckoo had flown the coop.

Where could the Pencil be? she wondered. *Or the Eraser? Or the Smudge?*

These last two were the other members of PUFF. She had named one the Eraser because he was so pink, and the other, affectionately, the Smudge, because he—if it was a he—was the messiest person Evangeline had ever seen. The Smudge was so messy in fact that Evangeline had never been entirely certain if the Smudge was a man animal nut or a woman animal nut.

Still wondering about PUFF, Evangeline set her bag on the doorstep.

Should I ring the doorbell? she asked herself. *Or simply open the door and walk in?*

But just as she was lifting her finger toward the bell, the door opened as if she had been expected. In front of Evangeline stood a boy, a boy who was taller than she but who appeared to be just about her own age. His hair was thick and brown and had been combed back in a way that you don't see most kids wearing their hair. His eyes were brown too, the color of caramel. But it wasn't the color of the boy's eyes that caught Evangeline off-guard; it was their expression. Evangeline decided they were just about the saddest eyes she had ever seen.

Behind him stood a man who was nearly as tall as her father. But there, all similarities stopped. If Evangeline hadn't promised to save the minks, she might have turned and run right back to the airport, even if it had meant sitting next to Libby Heck again on the trip back.

The man had long black hair that hung down in dark strands on either side of his face, giving the impression that he was leering out from shadows. Even though it was a warm day, he wore a hat—a hat made of a glistening black fur. And apparently the hat had a tail, because it hung down over the man's right shoulder, where it rested like a big black fuzzy snake. Under his large, crooked nose, a mustache sprouted. But like his hair, it was thin and lank. It reminded Evangeline of a sick bird, too unwell to escape from the horrible man upon whose lip it was trapped. His eyes were the color of coal. Unlike the boy's, they glistened with cruelty.

Evangeline shivered in spite of herself.

"Yes?" the man said, curling up the corners of his

mouth in what Evangeline supposed to be some kind of a smile. "Can I help you?"

You really mustn't blame Evangeline for what happened next. It was probably because she was frightened that she did what she did—frightened and confused. After all, she was expecting to see her father's second cousin, twice removed, or his wife, India Terpsichore. Instead, she had been surprised by the sad boy and the mysterious man with the black hat. And then there was PUFF's absence.

"Yes?" the man repeated. This time he did not bother to pretend to smile. "Can I help you?"

"My name is Libby," Evangeline said. "Libby . . . er . . . Rick."

Chapter 6

Baby Bubbles

Evangeline realized at once the foolhardiness of saying such a thing. Melvin and India Terpsichore knew that her name was Evangeline Mudd, not Libby Rick, or at least India Terpsichore did. Melvin never had gotten her name straight. He'd been too busy thinking about turning baby minks into jackets and bathing trunks and diapers and what the Pencil, the Eraser, and the Smudge were planning to do about it.

Yes, she knew it was a silly thing to do and, she was forced to admit to herself, it wasn't entirely honest. But there was something horrible about the man with the black hat—horrible and, she couldn't help but feel, dangerous. She simply couldn't bear for him to know her name.

To worsen matters, he now appeared to be studying her, narrowing his eyes as if, perhaps, he was thinking that he had met her before. But Evangeline was certain that she had never seen this man. He was the kind of person that she would never forget, no matter how much she might want to.

Neither boy nor man said a word, but the girl was determined that she would not be the first to speak.

I've already told one tremendous fib, she thought. *If I speak again, who knows what I might say?*

Evangeline distracted herself by concentrating on a smell that was wafting from the direction of where the man and boy stood. It was overpoweringly sweet, and not sweet like cookies baking but sweet like soap or cheap perfume. The smell seemed to carry her back to a time long, long ago.

Is it possible? she wondered, furrowing her brow to keep from sneezing. *Is it possible that I smell . . . Baby Bubbles?*

Baby Bubbles was the name of the bubble bath Magdalena used to pour into Evangeline's tub after a long day of brachiating. It was pink, the color of the phlox that grew in the garden at the cozy bungalow, and was sold in big jars. On the label was a picture of a fat, laughing baby sitting all alone in a tub.

Evangeline had always worried about that baby, since its mother or father was nowhere in sight. The longer Evangeline stood on the doorstep, the stronger that worrisome feeling returned.

Just when it seemed that the man in the black hat was going to say something, India Terpsichore came bounding by the open door.

"What's going on here?" the ballerina demanded of the man. She was wearing a lime green leotard, and though Evangeline didn't mean to, she immediately thought of those disgusting caterpillars that Merriweather was always horrified to find on his tomato plants.

"It's a girl, madam," the man replied in a voice somewhere between a whisper and a hiss.

"A *girl*?" India Terpsichore said the word the way you or I might say *flea*. She didn't so much as glance at Evangeline.

"She says her name is Libby Rick," said the man in a tone of voice that suggested he was not entirely convinced that Evangeline was telling the truth.

Up to now, the ballerina hadn't bothered to turn her head toward Evangeline.

"But I've never heard of a girl named Libby Rick," India Terpsichore whined, squatting and sticking her leg out to the side, as if she were hoping to trip someone.

"Nor have I, madam," whispered the man,

squinting at Evangeline.

Without warning, the ballerina jumped onto her toes and threw her arms in the air.

"She's probably come for my autograph," she squealed as she tippytoed around in a circle.

For the first time, she turned to look at Evangeline.

"India Terpsichore," said the girl. "I can explain, I—"

"Don't interrupt me," said India Terpsichore, even though she hadn't been saying anything at all and it was she who had interrupted Evangeline. "Didn't your parents teach you any manners?"

"But India Terpsichore, I—" Evangeline tried again, ignoring the remark that the horrid woman had made about her parents. (In fact, Merriweather and Magdalena had taught Evangeline excellent manners.)

"You remind me of someone," India Terpsichore interrupted again. She pushed her way past the man and the boy and bent down from the waist so that her long, bumpy nose practically raked Evangeline's. "You remind me of someone I used to know."

Could it be? thought Evangeline, stunned that India Terpsichore hadn't immediately caught her in her trick. *Could it be that she is so interested in herself that she's forgotten about me?*

"Yes," said India Terpsichore. "It's all coming back to me now. It was someone I didn't like. Now, who was it?"

Evangeline was right. And though it might sound a little surprising, it isn't really. Some people are like that. Some people are so focused on themselves that they don't see the world around them. All they see is themselves, and India Terpsichore was one of those people. India Terpsichore didn't recognize Evangeline because the truth is, she had never really looked at her in the first place.

"I have it now!" the ballerina finally shrieked. "It was that hideous relative of my husband. She had let herself go too. That's why you remind me of her. Now, what was her name?"

With a long, skinny finger, India Terpsichore began tapping her nose, first on one side, then the other, as if

Evangline's name were stuck in there and she were

hoping it would fall out.

The man in the black hat looked straight at Evangeline and smiled the way a wolf might just before it jumps on its victim from the high rock where it has been hiding.

"Perhaps it was *Evangeline,* madam," he said.

Chapter 7

The Ballerina Hall of Fame

It had been bad enough to hear India Terpsichore saying such untrue things about her, but when Evangeline heard the man with the drooping mustache utter her name, she felt a cold wind blow right through her. It was a good thing that she had already experienced the dangers of the Ikkinasti Jungle or she might have bolted. The girl looked straight ahead as if she had never heard the name *Evangeline* in her life. But in her heart of hearts, she was shaking.

He knows my name! It ricocheted like a handball from one side of her brain to another. *He knows my name!*

Maybe he has heard Melvin talking about me, she reasoned. But almost in the same second, she ruled it out since Melvin had never, not once in the three months she had spent at Mudd's Manor, called her by her proper name.

The horrible man continued to look at Evangeline, and for one wild minute, she let her imagination get the best of her.

He's a wizard! she thought. *He reads minds!*

This terrifying thought began to work on Evangeline, making her feel that she had lost before she had even begun. But just when she was about to turn and make a run for it, she saw a shadow pass through the coldness of the man's eyes. It retreated just as quickly as it had advanced, but Evangeline saw it just as surely as she saw the man himself, and she recognized it for what it was—disappointment, disappointment that when he had spat out her name like a dart, a dart targeting Evangeline herself, she had not squirmed or shouted or gasped. It was that glint of disappointment that allowed Evangeline to carry on through all that was to follow.

"Evangeleeeen!" shouted India Terpsichore, leaping up and nearly landing on the girl. "I knew I'd think of it. Evangeleeeeen. Yes! Oh, she was a poor thing. I tried to help her. I did! But what could I do? I am only one person, and one person, no matter how fabulous, cannot do much."

This was a ridiculous thing to say, and Evangeline knew it. It was untrue too. India Terpsichore had done nothing at all to help Evangeline when she had been forced to stay there while her parents were in Ikkinasti. In fact, the horrid woman had made the girl's life much worse. Besides, Evangeline knew very well that one person *can* do almost anything. And the person doesn't have to be fabulous either. The person can be ordinary, as ordinary as you or me.

If the situation had been different, Evangeline would have told India Terpsichore just how wrong she was. But this was not the time to have a philosophical argument. This was a time to say as little as possible and to keep your eyes wide open.

The man spoke again. This time he wasn't smiling.

"And if I may be so bold, Ms. Libby Rick," he said with a sneer, "what is it that you are doing here?"

"Good question," India Terpsichore piped. "A very good question. I was just about to ask it myself."

"The . . . er . . . the committee sent me," Evangeline announced.

"The committee?" the man repeated.

"Yes. The committee . . . um . . . the committee from the Ballerina Hall of Fame. It's . . . it's like the Baseball Hall of Fame except that it's for ballerinas."

Later, Evangeline wondered where the idea to say such a thing had come from. Certainly, she hadn't been planning to say it. It was almost as if the words had been there all along, hanging around in her mouth waiting until just that moment to make a break for freedom. In the end, she decided that it must have been the result of the training her parents had given her.

"In order to survive in the Ikkinasti Jungle," her father had often said, "a golden-hair must be able to think quickly on her feet."

"He's right, darling," her mother had added. "The jungle doesn't give one time for hemming and hawing. The young ape who hesitates when facing the welcoming grin of a crocodile may soon find herself in the less welcoming space of the crocodile's tummy."

The man in the black hat may not be a crocodile, Evangeline thought later, *but he is the closest human thing to it.*

India Terpsichore leaped up like a rocket.

"The Ballerina Hall of Fame?" she squealed, landing with a thud.

"Congratulations!" said Evangeline, now warming to her story. "I've been sent to . . . uh . . . make a report."

"I don't believe I've ever heard of the Ballerina Hall

41

of Fame," said the man with the black hat. From the way he was looking at Evangeline, he might as well have said, "You're lying, and I know it!"

"Of course, you haven't," India Terpsichore snapped, wheeling around to face the man. "And do you know why?"

"Why, madam?" the man asked, with that same slight bow of his head that he always performed when he spoke to India Terpsichore.

"Because you are not a once-famous ballerina who has not let herself go," she sniped.

She turned directly to Evangeline and grabbed the girl's shoulders with her long, skinny hands.

"You will stay here, naturally," she said in a wheedling voice, yanking Evangeline across the threshold and into the house. "That way, you'll get to know me better, you lucky girl."

She turned to the man with the black hat.

"Of course, you have met Alexy Alexy?"

Evangeline's heart nearly stopped beating. The man with the black hat was Alexy Alexy, the world's highest-jumping ballet dancer? She didn't know what she had been expecting, not that she had been expecting anything at all, but not this man with his hissing voice and his cruel eyes.

"It's . . . it's nice to meet you," she forced herself to say to the man.

"Not him, you silly goose," said India Terpsichore. *"Him!"*

And she pointed to the boy with the sad brown eyes.

Chapter 8

Look Out Below!

"You?" Evangeline said before she could stop herself. "But you're only a boy."

But before Alexy could respond, the man with the drooping mustache tightened his grip on the boy's shoulders and pushed him down the corridor.

"It's time for practice," he whispered.

Evangeline wasn't sure whether it was her imagination or not, but when Alexy Alexy looked back, she thought she saw a tear slide from the boy's cheek and drop to the cold marble floor.

In the meantime, India Terpsichore was talking a mile a minute.

"We'll start at the beginning," she prattled. "With my baby pictures."

But Evangeline's mind was elsewhere.

"Excuse me," she said. "But who is that man with Alexy Alexy?"

"Ratsputin?" replied the ballerina, making no attempt to hide her irritation that the question had not been about *her*. "He's Alexy's guardian and dance master. He travels everywhere with him."

"But what about Alexy's parents?"

"Let me remind you, Libby Rick," barked India Terpsichore with an ugly sneer, "that the committee sent you here to talk about *me*! Forget about that dreadful boy. Now, where was I? Oh yes, my childhood. I never really took a first step, you know. I took a first *leap*. Like this!"

India Terpsichore suddenly sprang down the corridor. Unfortunately, her husband, Melvin Mudd, chief executive officer of Mudd's Marvelous Minks, was just rounding the corner at the very spot where the ballerina was planning to land.

"Look out below!" she cried.

"Not again!" Melvin shouted.

But it was too late.

In the end, it was Evangeline who had to untangle

them. India Terpsichore's left foot had become hope-
lessly wedged behind her husband's right shoulder,
and Melvin had his wife in a kind of one-armed
hammerlock.

I ought to just leave them all knotted up like this,

Evangeline thought. *Then the minks would be safe forever.*

As the girl worked, lifting this leg here, shifting that arm there, she had the uncomfortable feeling that her father's second cousin, twice removed, was watching her closely.

This is it, she thought. *Melvin knows who I am.*

When the two were finally separated and standing, Melvin Mudd turned to Evangeline.

"Thank you, Emmelina," he said, buttoning the jacket of his suit. "Long time no see."

Evangeline sighed and looked down at the floor.

"Melvin," she began.

But once again India Terpsichore's vanity saved her.

"Emmelina?" The ballerina pouted. "What are you talking about? This is Libby Rick."

She lifted her leg and pointed to Evangeline with her toe, very nearly clipping the tip of Evangeline's nose. Evangeline stepped backward into the shadows of the hallway.

"Libby Rick?" said Melvin. "Funny. I thought she was Emmelina somebody or other. . . ."

"You can *think* she is the Countess of Nonnynonnybooboo," India Terpsichore sniffed. "But the truth is that she is Libby Rick from the

Ballerina Hall of Fame. And she thinks I'm fabulous, don't you, Libby Rick?"

"Er . . ." said Evangeline, putting her hand behind her back and crossing her fingers. "Yes."

Melvin took one final look at her, turned on his heel, and walked down the hall.

"Odd," he muttered. "I was sure she was Evangelica somebody or other."

The crisis had passed. Melvin, like his wife, was so self-involved that he hadn't really recognized her. She could have been the Easter Bunny as far as he was concerned. It's a good thing she wasn't, though. He might have turned her into a jacket.

Evangeline had just breathed a sigh of relief at her good fortune, if it is good fortune to have such beastly relatives, when Melvin suddenly whirled around.

"Hey, Libby Rick! You haven't seen any animal nuts hanging around here, have you?" he shouted. "They're up to something, Libby Rick. They're up to something."

Melvin jerked his head to the side as if he were expecting an animal nut to come busting out of the wall.

"They're everywhere!" he whispered.

Evangeline noticed that he was sweating profusely.

"But don't you worry," he continued, tapping his

temple with his index finger. "It takes more than a couple of animal nuts to outsmart Melvin Mudd."

He turned once more and moved down the hall in a way that reminded Evangeline of one of those snakes that travels on its side instead of straight ahead on its belly.

In the meantime, India Terpsichore was yawning and tapping her foot.

"Libby Rick," she finally said. "Let's talk about something interesting. Me, for example."

As India Terpsichore led her away, the girl's mind raced with questions.

Where are B. Eversharp and the Eraser?

Where is the Smudge?

How am I going to find out the location of the mink farm?

Why did Alexy look so sad?

But there was one question that troubled her more than any of the others. It rode through her mind again and again, like a frightened horse stuck on a carousel, and each time it passed by, Evangeline felt a chill settle into her spine.

How did Ratsputin know my name?

For now, of course, there was no chance of getting any of these questions answered. For now, the only thing she could do was nod and try to look interested as India Terpsichore pranced down the corridor, shouting, "Look at me, Libby Rick! Look at me!"

Chapter 9

A Spy in the House

When Evangeline awoke the next morning, far later than she had planned, her ears were still ringing with the horrible whine of the ballerina's voice.

"This is me the day I was born," India Terpsichore had begun, handing Evangeline a dog-eared photograph from the top of a teetering stack.

But when Evangeline looked at the photograph, she nearly screamed.

That's not a baby, the girl thought. *It's one of those wrinkly Chinese dogs all wrapped up in a pink blanket.*

As she inspected the photograph more closely,

however, she realized it couldn't be one of those wrinkly Chinese dogs, because those wrinkly Chinese dogs were about a million times cuter than the purple-faced thing that was squalling its head off in the picture.

One after another the photos came, each more horrible than the last. Evangeline was desperate. Looking at the pictures of India Terpsichore wasn't getting her a bit closer to discovering the location of Melvin Mudd's mink ranch and, in fact, was clouding her mind with image after image of the horrible ballerina.

She had been hoping to run into Melvin again. She was already developing a plan that might trick him into revealing where the minks were hidden. But when he learned that his wife was getting out her baby pictures, the CEO developed a mysterious headache and ran out of the room.

She had also hoped she might see Alexy Alexy one more time before the evening was over, but, like

Melvin, both he and Ratsputin had disappeared.

Evangeline hopped out of bed and ran to the window. The sun had been up for hours, but B. Eversharp and the other members of PUFF were nowhere to be seen.

"They should be here by now, " she said.

Turning from the window, Evangeline froze in her tracks. There, lying on the rug just in front of the door, was a plain white envelope.

It wasn't there last night, she told herself. *I'm sure of it.*

Before she went to bed, she had done a hundred jumping jacks in that very spot, trying to shake the image of baby India Terpsichore, which she was afraid had burned into her very brain.

There's only one explanation, Evangeline quickly concluded. *Someone shoved the envelope under the door after I went to bed.*

She picked up the envelope and turned it over. A faint scent of lilacs wafted through the room.

"B. Eversharp!" Evangeline whispered.

Tucking the envelope into her pajama top, she ran to the closet. (By the way, a good closet is one of the only places you should read a letter that mysteriously appears in the middle of the night.) Once safely inside, she turned on the light and took out the envelope. Her heart pounded through her pajamas when she read the note that was inside.

Dear Evangeline,

Thank goodness you have arrived. We knew you would come, and for this we thank you from the bottom of our hearts. But, dear girl, we have some rather unfortunate news. That hideous woman is planning to dance on a baby elephant. A baby! Our sister organization, AAPT (Animals Are People Too), was going to locate the baby and save it, but they have been called away to rescue a laboratory mouse.

As of yet, we don't know where Melvin Mudd has hidden this baby elephant. Naturally, we must do everything we can to find out so that we can stop it. This means, of course, that we can provide very little assistance in freeing the minks. I'm afraid, dear, you are on your own.

B. Eversharp

For some reason, B. Eversharp had tucked a picture of the Smudge inside the envelope. He—or was it *she*? Evangeline wondered—was standing in front of Mudd's Manor. Half of his—or was it *her*?—shirttails were tucked in; the other half were flapping in the wind. It did Evangeline good to see her old friend, but the girl did not allow herself more than a moment to reminisce. Right now there were other things to think about.

Of course, the Pencil was right. PUFF had to save the baby elephant from India Terpsichore's enormous feet. On the other hand, how could she possibly save the minks by herself before Melvin turned them into jackets?

If it had been me sitting on the floor of that closet, I know exactly what I would have done. I would have spent a long time feeling sorry for myself and thinking things like, *That's it! I might as well pack up and go home*. Evangeline, however, was not the kind of girl who gave up so easily. If she were, she never could have saved her parents from the dangers of the Ikkinasti Jungle.

She rested her elbow on her knee and her head on her hand.

The first thing I've got to do, she reasoned, *is go down and get some breakfast.*

As if to confirm, her stomach rumbled.

She didn't have a concrete plan yet, but in order to get one, she would need energy, and energy, in this case, meant breakfast. And so, to Evangeline's way of thinking, breakfast was the first small step in getting a plan.

Evangeline remembered something her father had often told her. "Golden-hairs are nothing if they aren't practical," she could hear him say in his fine deep voice. "'First things first' is the way they live, and it's a very good way to live, indeed."

For a second or two, it was almost as if he and Magdalena were sitting there in the closet with her, and in a way, I suppose, they were. When she closed her eyes, she could feel their warmth and their love and their good humor enveloping her. This brought the girl immense comfort. There was something else that comforted her, too, something important. The letter itself.

If it wasn't here when I went to bed, but it was *here when I woke up, that can only mean one thing. PUFF must have a spy in the house.*

She had no idea who it was, of course, and perhaps she never would, but the very fact that there was someone besides her in Mudd's Manor who was against the terrible plans of Melvin Mudd and his wife emboldened Evangeline.

"I will save those minks," she said aloud. "I will!"

She stood up and opened the door. And then without quite knowing why, she added, "And while I'm at it, I'll find out why Alexy Alexy is so sad, and if I can, I'll help him too!"

Chapter 10

Chocolate Parfait!

Evangeline dressed quickly and made her way down the hall to the grand staircase, but long before she got to the bottom of the steps, she discovered that Mudd's Manor was bustling.

Ballet dancers whizzed back and forth, flitting from room to room like butterflies in a hurricane. Musicians—violinists and violists, trumpeters and trombonists, bassists and bassoonists—were plunking and peeping and tooting and tweeting and, in general, creating such a ruckus that Evangeline was forced to put her fingers in her ears. There were even unicyclists—three of them, Evangeline decided, though it was difficult to tell from her vantage point on the

steps. They popped in and out of doorways and cut around corners without the slightest regard for anyone who might be in their way.

Evangeline had no idea what it might feel like to be run over by a unicycle, and she didn't want to find out. Still, she had to make it into the kitchen.

Maybe if I flatten myself against a wall and scootch down the hallway, she thought.

She had just decided to make a run for it when the front door swung open so forcefully that she was surprised the hinges hadn't popped their screws and sent the door hurtling through the air like a roof in a tornado. It was not a mighty wind that had opened the door, however. It was a mighty woman.

Evangeline knew it wasn't polite to stare, but she couldn't help herself. The woman was so tall that had she straightened her powerful neck, her head would almost certainly have touched the top of the door frame. And that wasn't all—that head was completely bald! In the morning light, it glistened like a ball of ice and caused Evangeline to squint as she continued to gape.

"Silence!" the giant woman roared in a basso profundo.

It seemed to Evangeline that someone had pressed the mute button on the world's most powerful remote. Whereas before she had been forced to put her fingers in her ears, now the only sound she could hear was the tinkling of the crystals on the chandelier as it rocked dangerously on its golden chain.

The dancers stopped their cavorting in midair and contorted themselves like human pretzels, doing everything they could, it seemed, to land as silently on the manor's polished floors as dragonflies might on blades of grass. The musicians abandoned their scales and musical phrases midnote and hung their instruments beside them or hid them behind their backs.

"Who is that?" Evangeline whispered to a ballerina who was standing at attention in front of her.

"You don't know?" the ballerina whispered back, trying not to move her lips lest she call attention to herself from the terrifying giantess. "It's Chocolate Parfait!"

Evangeline thought that perhaps the racket the musicians had been making just a few minutes earlier had temporarily caused her ears not to work properly. It almost sounded as if the ballerina had said the woman's name was *Chocolate Parfait*!

"She's creating the costumes for *Hansel and Gretel in Kaboomistan,*" the dancer continued. "She's here to take our measurements."

"Silence!" Chocolate Parfait roared again, raising her arm in the air like a cannon. "How do you expect me to design mink tutus and mink tuxedos and mink everything else with all this racket?"

With one giant step, Chocolate Parfait cleared the entryway and was into the house, tall and solid as an oak tree.

"Tweed!" she bellowed. "Tell them to line up!"

From behind Chocolate Parfait there appeared a woman almost as short as the costume designer was tall. This woman seemed to have found all the hair that the larger woman had gotten rid of. Under all the waves and curls billowing over her head like rapids over a boulder, it was practically impossible to see a face.

"Miss Parfait requests that you form an orderly line," Tweed squeaked. "Er . . . single file would be best."

But it had been unnecessary to say anything at all.

The musicians and dancers had already formed a line, which, in the end, snaked in and out of the great room, and the library, and the dining room, and the den, and every room except the kitchen. They had done this as quietly as dust floating in a ray of sunlight. Even the unicyclists, who were last, were behaving themselves.

The only person who had not jumped into the line, besides Chocolate Parfait and Tweed, of course, was Evangeline, who stood on the bottom step of the stairway as still as a statue in a garden.

It wasn't just that she was mesmerized by Chocolate Parfait and her peculiar assistant; it was what their presence in Mudd's Manor meant. If the time had come to measure the performers for their costumes, that could only mean one thing. The minks were running out of time.

I have to find that mink farm, the girl told herself. *I have to! Before it's too late.*

But Evangeline's thoughts were interrupted when she discovered that Chocolate Parfait was eyeing her up and down, the way a butcher might scrutinize a slab of beef while deciding if he should turn it into hamburger or steak.

"We'll start with her, Tweed!" she bugled.

And before Evangeline had a chance to protest, the costumer whipped a yellow tape measure out of her pocket and snapped it in the air the way a cowboy snaps his rawhide at a roundup of the dogies. With a flick of the wrist, she pinched it around

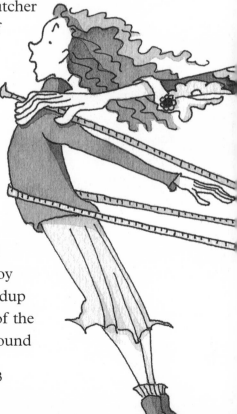

Evangeline's neck so tight that the girl felt that the top of her head might pop off.

"Twelve and a half inches," Chocolate Parfait shouted.

"Twelve and a half!" Tweed repeated, scratching the numbers down in a yellow notebook.

In less than a minute, it was over. By the time the costumer had finished, Evangeline had been yanked, jerked, prodded, and poked with an energy so forceful that it left her feeling as if she *had* been run over by a unicycle.

At one point during the whirlwind, Chocolate Parfait spun her around, and Evangeline thought that she had actually been able to see Tweed's eyes under the cascade of bangs that rushed over the woman's forehead. Evangeline noted that the expression there was surprisingly sympathetic, but it had all happened so quickly there was no way to be sure.

"Next!" Chocolate Parfait bellowed, shoving Evangeline out of her way with one hand.

Dizzy and sore as she was, Evangeline didn't waste another second. Still thinking about the minks, she made a dash for the kitchen door.

Chapter 11

Nine o'Clock. Tonight.

Once safely in the kitchen, Evangeline was again overcome by the powerful scent of Baby Bubbles. It was as strong, or stronger even, than it had been on the doorstep when she had first noticed it. The second thing she noted was that the only two people in the kitchen were Alexy Alexy, who was sitting at the table, and, standing behind him like a dragon guarding his loot, the dance master.

Because the door through which Evangeline had entered was to their backs, and because there was so much going on in the rest of the house, neither Alexy Alexy nor Ratsputin noticed Evangeline's arrival.

"Eat!" Ratsputin was saying to the boy. "You've got to eat!"

"But I've already eaten," Alexy Alexy answered, and from the look of the table, Evangeline believed him.

Empty cereal bowls sat next to plates on which the remnants of pancakes might have been the forlorn pieces of forgotten jigsaw puzzles. There were other plates too, plates with just the tiniest bit of egg left over, and plates with bacon crumbs and ham rinds and toast crusts and sausage ends and, well, the remains of just every possible breakfasty thing that you might think of. It looked as if a crew of very hungry lumberjacks had eaten breakfast at that table.

Still, Ratsputin pushed another stack of pancakes and a rasher of bacon in front of Alexy Alexy.

"I said eat!" he snarled.

Now, some of you might have

grandmothers who encourage you to eat. And even though you are stuffed to the very top of your head with all the terrific things they have prepared with only you in mind, and even though you have eaten until you feel you are going to explode, "Eat!" they shout. "You've hardly touched a morsel!"

The reason for this behavior is simple. They love you! They think, rightly or wrongly, that the more you eat, the bigger you'll grow, and the bigger you grow, the more of you there will be for them to love. When they tell you to eat, it really is just a way of saying "I love you more than you could possibly realize."

But when Ratsputin ordered Alexy to eat, there was not an ounce of love in it, and it was clear to Evangeline, from the way the dreadful man's hand clasped the boy's shoulder, like the talon of a falcon gripping a rabbit it had just snatched out of its hole, there was no choice. Alexy would have to eat the pancakes.

"You'll never make it to thirty feet if you don't have energy," Ratsputin hissed.

"I don't want to make it to thirty feet," Alexy said as he picked up a piece of the bacon.

"You're a quitter," Ratsputin jeered. "Just like your parents!"

For a moment, from the way his shoulders tensed,

Evangeline thought that Alexy Alexy was going to jump up from the table and confront his guardian and dance master. She very much wanted him to, but before he could do anything at all, Melvin Mudd, chief executive officer of Mudd's Marvelous Minks and her father's second cousin, twice removed, came bounding in from the door on the other side of the room.

"Morning, Libby Rick!" he called out.

It irritated Evangeline to no end that when she was living at Mudd's Manor before, Melvin had never, not once, called her by her actual name. It was always Angelica, or Emmelina, or Eglantine or something— never, never Evangeline. The maddening thing was that now that he thought her name was Libby Rick, he got it right every single time.

But the girl could not spare even a second to think about such things because when Ratsputin heard Melvin Mudd greet her, he wheeled around and saw her for the first time since she had entered the kitchen.

Evangeline had seen pictures of cobras watching their prey just before they were about to strike. This was the look that Ratsputin was giving her now. She wouldn't have been a bit surprised to see a forked tongue flick out from between the man's cruel lips.

But frightened as she was, Evangeline met Ratsputin's

gaze with one of her own, remembering, as she did so, Magdalena's advice.

"Survival in the jungle comes down to a few simple rules," her mother had said. "And one of those rules, Evangeline darling, is never, never act like prey, even if you think you might *be* one."

The dance master turned his back to her.

"Whatdaya think about those animal nuts now, Libby Rick?" asked the chief executive officer. "I tricked 'em! They'd do anything to stop *Hansel and Gretel in Kaboomistan.* That's why I'm keeping everything about it top secret, and that's why everybody is staying right here at Mudd's Manor until opening night. The dancers, the orchestra, and all the others. Everybody! They got here early this morning. Probably before those animal nuts were even out of bed!

"That's not the only trick up my sleeve, either," Melvin muttered to himself as he circled around the table. "Not by a long shot. Those animal nuts might think that I'm an idiot, but I'm not. No sirree, Bob!"

Suddenly Melvin stopped in his tracks.

"Wait a minute," he shouted, jerking his head to one side as if something had suddenly flown into one ear and banged against the inside of the other. "Wait a minute!"

Melvin began to emit a series of low snorting noises, like a pig rooting in the mud for the end of a turnip. It took Evangeline a few seconds to realize that this was Melvin's version of laughter.

"Maybe I am," he coughed out between snorts. "Maybe that's *just* what I am. A *blooming* idiot! Get it? Get it, Libby Rick? A *blooming* idiot!"

Evangeline had no idea what Melvin found so hilarious, but he fell into a fit of such snorting that at one point she considered that she might have to pound him on the back. Eventually, however, Melvin did calm down just as Ratsputin, who had regarded Melvin with the same surprise as Evangeline, yanked Alexy's chair out from the table.

"Come," the dance master ordered. "You've got to practice."

He pulled the boy from the table and led him toward the door.

Evangeline wanted to speak to Alexy Alexy, to say anything to let him know that he had a friend in her.

"Good luck, Alexy," she called out. "Practicing, I mean."

Ratsputin turned to her once more; once more he reminded her of a cobra.

"Luck?" he hissed. "Alexy doesn't *need* luck!"

He turned away so rapidly that the tail on the black

hat circumscribed a half circle in the air and fell helplessly onto his back. He pushed the boy roughly, perhaps more roughly than he had meant to show, out the door, but not before Alexy Alexy had a chance to look back at Evangeline and point upward toward the second floor of the house.

The girl remained expressionless as she read the words that formed silently on Alexy's lips.

"Nine o'clock. Tonight."

"A blooming idiot," Melvin Mudd snorted, turning toward the window. "That's a good one!"

Chapter 12

A Terrible Mistake

"Nine o'clock. Tonight," Evangeline repeated to herself. What could Alexy have meant? The way he had pointed upstairs seemed to mean that he wanted to meet her there.

In the meantime, she was alone in the kitchen with her father's second cousin, twice removed. Melvin Mudd by now was over his private joke, whatever it was, and was standing on his tiptoes with his nose pressed up against the window over the sink. First he jerked his head way over to the left, and then, as if he had caught something out of the corner of his eye, he yanked it way over to the right. He reminded her of a hyena she had once seen in a zoo.

If he keeps that up, Evangeline thought, *he is going to get a stiff neck.*

Melvin was muttering to himself. Every now and again Evangeline heard the words *animal nuts.*

This was just the chance the girl had been waiting for.

"Um . . . excuse me, Melvin," she began.

"Yes, Libby Rick? What is it?"

He turned to face Evangeline, who couldn't help but notice that her father's second cousin, twice removed, had developed a twitch in his left eyebrow.

"I was just thinking," Evangeline continued, trying hard not to stare at the eyebrow, which now was squirming like a worm on a hook. "It must be very difficult to be the chief executive officer of a *big, important* corporation like Mudd's Marvelous Minks."

The effect of this sentence on Melvin was tremendous. He tensed his shoulders and leaned forward. He cocked his head and cupped his hand behind his ear. The eyebrow nearly jumped off his forehead.

"What was that you said, Libby Rick?" he whispered. "I didn't quite catch it. I think it was something about *big* and *important.*"

He was practically drooling.

"It must be a terribly difficult job," she continued. "Turning minks into jackets, I mean."

73

Melvin suddenly slumped forward and almost fell into the chair opposite Evangeline's. The eyebrow quivered as if someone had tickled it.

"Oh, Libby Rick," the man whined. "You have no idea!"

Evangeline marveled at how easily Melvin was falling into her trap. Neither Merriweather nor Magdalena, she knew, would ever be fooled so easily.

Melvin propped his elbows on the table and grabbed his head with both hands.

"I'm a *good* person, Libby Rick," he declared. "I am! Just because I turn minks into jackets and diapers and hats and swimming trunks and baseball uniforms and wedding gowns and pajamas and tuxedos and handkerchiefs and napkins and boxer shorts and blankets and bathrobes, does that make me a bad person?"

"Rich ladies and gentlemen have very delicate noses," Evangeline said. "Why should they use a scratchy tissue if they can afford a mink hanky from Mudd's Marvelous Minks?"

Evangeline could hardly believe that she was speaking such nonsense. It was even worse than telling India Terpsichore that she was fabulous.

Melvin lifted his head and slammed both his hands on the table.

"Libby Rick!" he exclaimed. "You have pinned the tail right on the donkey! It's the same with mink baseball uniforms! Rich ladies and gentlemen like to play baseball just like everyone else. Why shouldn't they do it in mink?"

Evangeline wanted to tell Melvin that he should ask the minks that question, but Melvin didn't expect an answer. He jumped up from the table and ran back to his place at the window.

"The animal nuts even want to stop *Hansel and Gretel in Kaboomistan*! And why? Simply because the tutus and leotards will be mink!" he shouted.

And now Evangeline made a terrible mistake. A mistake that could have ruined everything.

"What about that baby elephant?" she said. "Don't forget about that."

The second the words left her mouth, the girl's heart practically stopped beating. As far as she knew, Melvin knew nothing about PUFF's plan to save the baby elephant from India Terpsichore's enormous feet, and now she had practically told him. He would wonder how she knew there was an elephant. But she hadn't been able to stop herself. It was terribly difficult to pretend to be someone named Libby Rick and say crazy things about mink hankies without making a mistake.

For a moment, Melvin said nothing. Evangeline wondered if he had even heard her. But just when she decided that perhaps he hadn't, he wheeled around on the rubber heels of his shiny black shoes, causing them to screech against the marble floor like the tires of a fast-moving car whose driver had suddenly slammed on the brakes.

"What was that you said, Libby Rick?" he demanded. The eyebrow was hopping around like a Mexican jumping bean. "What was that you said about the baby elephant?"

It's all over, Evangeline said to herself. *I've ruined everything.*

In the flash of a second, the girl saw herself back in a plane heading toward the cozy bungalow. The gravity in the room doubled, tripled, quadrupled. Evangeline felt as if she were on one of the planets where it was impossible to lift your foot off the ground.

"What a brilliant idea, Libby Rick!" Melvin exclaimed, practically suffocating Evangeline as he threw his arms around her. "Brilliant. I'll dress the baby elephant in mink too!"

Later, Evangeline wondered if it was her relief at not having been discovered or the fact that Melvin was squeezing the life out of her that made her feel that she was going to faint. Perhaps it was the overpowering smell of cigar smoke that permeated Melvin's expensive Italian suit.

Melvin finally released his grip.

"I owe you one, Libby Rick!" he shouted as he walked in circles around the table. "I owe you one for that idea. You just let me know if there's anything I can ever do for you."

Evangeline couldn't believe how her luck had turned. One second, she was sure that she had been discovered. The next, Melvin was promising that he'd do anything for her.

This is it, she thought. *It's now or never.*

"Actually, Melvin, there is one little thing," she said, looking down at the table and picking up a grain of spilled salt with the tip of her finger.

"You just name it, Libby Rick. You just name it."

"You see," she began slowly. "I've never actually been to a mink farm."

Melvin stopped in his tracks. Evangeline looked up just in time to see his right eyebrow join the left in a series of twitches that made it look like they were dancing with each other.

"You—you—you don't mean that you would like to visit the mink ranch, do you, Libby Rick?" he stammered. "You don't mean that, do you?"

There was no going back now.

"Actually," Evangeline said. "I do."

Melvin hunched his shoulders. He stood as still as a tenpin when the bowling alley is closed. To Evangeline, it seemed as if Melvin were going to stand there forever, like a fairy-tale character who had been turned to stone. But finally, the man relaxed his shoulders and stood straight up.

"Well, what the hey, Libby Rick?" he practically shouted. "Why not? It's—"

"Mellllllllllllllllllllllllllllllvin!"

India Terpsichore's voice cut the air like a sharp knife—slicing the moment right down the middle, Evangeline later thought, leaving Melvin on one side and her on the other.

"Mellllllllllllllllllllllllllllllvin!"

"Oooops! Gotta go!" Melvin called over his shoulder as he ran out the back door. "Nice talking to you, Libby Rick."

The door slammed behind him, as emphatic and final as an exclamation point at the end of a very short sentence.

Chapter 13

Twenty-nine Feet, Eleven Inches

There was no arguing it. Evangeline had missed her chance. And it was all because of India Terpsichore, who, for the rest of the day, refused to let the girl out of her sight. On several occasions, Evangeline tried to slip away, but the ballerina hunted her down like a cat after a cunning mouse, a mouse whose name was Libby Rick.

I've spent one whole day at Mudd's Manor, she told herself as she picked at the dinner India Terpsichore had prepared for her— five bean sprouts and a cracker—*but I'm not one step closer to finding the location of Melvin's mink farm. And with Chocolate Parfait and Tweed at work, the poor minks are closer than ever to becoming tutus and tuxedos.*

Evangeline knew better than to engage in this kind of thinking, but she couldn't help herself. With her constant showing off, India Terpsichore—who, at present, had one foot on the table and was twisting her waist around in a way that made it seem she was trying to unscrew her top half from her bottom half — had temporarily sucked away the girl's natural reserves of optimism.

This must be what honeybees feel like, Evangeline sighed to herself as she picked up a bean sprout, *when they return to the hive after a day's work and discover that someone has stolen all the honey.*

But then came a thought that shocked Evangeline into action.

What if she were still at Mudd's Manor when her baby brother or sister were born? Evangeline felt it was her sacred duty to be one of the first to welcome Fabiano or Pamelia or Bikita, or whoever it was going to be, into the world, and she was not the kind of girl to take a sacred duty lightly. She was absolutely determined to be there with her mother and father on the happy occasion. Evangeline felt her energy returning as surely as if someone were pouring honey right back into that honeycomb.

After all, she told herself, pushing her chair back to the kitchen table, *if I can go into the dangerous jungles of Ikkinasti, I can certainly find out where a mink farm is.*

Evangeline now turned her attention to the mysterious message from Alexy Alexy. What had the boy meant? There was no way of knowing, of course, but one thing was certain—he'd wanted to keep it a secret from his guardian and dance master, Ratsputin.

Throughout the day, Evangeline had kept a sharp lookout for him, but she'd seen neither boy nor man since the scene at the breakfast table. She turned to the wife of her father's second cousin, twice removed.

"Excuse me, India Terpsichore," she said. "But I was wondering if you might know where Alexy Alexy is."

"Where do you *think* he is, Libby Rick?" she snapped in that same irritated tone of voice she used when any conversation veered away from *her.* "He's practicing. That's what Alexy Alexy *does.* Ratsputin has some foolish idea that if Alexy would only put his mind to it, he could jump thirty feet."

Evangeline recalled the conversation she had heard earlier that day.

"Thirty feet!" she exclaimed. "But that's impossible!"

"Is it?" India Terpsichore barked, setting herself into a spin so that she spat out the next sentence in fragments, one fragment for each revolution. "So far . . .

the little brat . . . has made it . . . to . . . twenty-nine feet . . . eleven inches."

The ballerina stopped twirling and faced Evangeline, who was beginning to think of her as some kind of human top.

"But that's enough about that stupid boy," India Terpsichore panted. "The night is young, Libby Rick. Let's go over those photographs again."

Evangeline glanced up at the clock. Eight forty-five.

"I'd love to, of course," she stalled. "But . . . er . . . I think I'd better go up to my room. I need to . . . uh . . . write up my first report for the committee."

Evangeline left the kitchen and walked toward the stairs, but India Terpsichore was right behind, sticking to her closer than her own shadow. She followed Evangeline to the bottom of the steps.

"You'll be sure to put it in your report, won't you, Libby Rick?" she asked, pushing out her bottom lip. "You won't forget, will you?"

Evangeline had no idea what the woman was talking about.

"Forget?" Evangeline responded. "Forget what?"

"To tell them that I haven't let myself go," India Terpsichore said. "To tell them that I look fabulous."

Evangeline turned to face the woman. After a day of whirling and prancing and preening and leaping and kicking and bragging, the ballerina looked, well, she looked just about the way *you* would if you had been up to such antics.

Evangeline suddenly missed her own mother very much.

"No, India Terpsichore," she said as she turned around and made her way up the stairs to her room. "I won't forget."

Chapter 14

Tap-tappity-tap. Tap-tappity-tap.
*Tap-tappity-tap-tap-**tap!***

Once in her room, Evangeline sat on the edge of her bed. It was still a few minutes before nine o'clock.

"What was that stupid joke Melvin kept laughing about this morning?" she said aloud. "A blooming idiot. A blooming idiot."

She repeated this phrase many times, as if the repetition would wear it down, forcing it to reveal its truth. But try as she might, she couldn't understand the joke.

Next she tried to work out a problem that had been bothering her from the minute she had told Ratsputin that her name was Libby Rick. You see, all her life

Evangeline had tried to be an honest girl. She had done her best to practice the virtues that her beloved mother and father had worked so hard to instill in her.

"Honesty is the best policy," Merriweather had always said.

"He's right, you know," Magdalena had added.

But now, the girl thought, *here I am telling everybody that my name is Libby Rick and that I am from the Ballerina Hall of Fame. What would Merriweather say? Would Magdalena have done the same if she had been in my situation? And even if she had, would that make it okay? Is honesty always the best policy?*

For a moment, Evangeline considered the possibility of telling the truth, of going back downstairs and telling India Terpsichore who she really was.

But if I do that, the girl pondered, *I'll have to leave Mudd's Manor, and if that happens, how will I ever save the minks? Which is more important? Saving the minks or telling the truth?*

These questions circled her brain as if they had been caught in a whirlpool. Around and around they went, faster and faster, until it was impossible to tell one from the next. They would have to be answered one day, but before they could spin completely out of control, there came a tapping at the window.

Evangeline glanced at the china clock on the dresser. Nine o'clock exactly.

"Alexy Alexy!" she whispered.

But then she realized that would have been impossible. After all, her room was on the second floor. The tapping must have come from a branch of one of the trees that grew close to the house. But when the tapping repeated itself in exactly the same rhythm, she sprang up from the bed and ran to the window.

Cupping her hands against the glass, she peered out into the darkness. At first, it seemed there was nothing there but the black of night. But by and by, a face began to appear on the other side of the glass—first just the tip of a nose, like a tiny moon racing in its orbit, coming directly at her. Then a pair of lips, and finally, with almost astronomical quickness, two eyes peered at her through the windowpane. Those eyes! Alexy Alexy!

She threw open the window. The boy

hopped in from where he had been balancing on the ledge.

"What took you so long?" he asked. "Didn't you hear me?"

"But . . ." she stammered. "But how . . . ?"

"I jumped," Alexy said.

"You jumped?" Evangeline exclaimed. She looked out the window to the ground far below. "No one can jump that high."

"I can," Alexy Alexy whispered.

Now, if you or I could jump from the ground and land on the ledge of a second-story window, I'll bet we would tell everybody we knew. *Look what I can do!* we'd shout. *Isn't it fantastic? Isn't it great? Isn't it the coolest thing ever?* But the way Alexy Alexy said "I can," so softly that you could barely hear him, wasn't at all like that. It was more like he was telling you the saddest thing he knew.

"I can," he repeated. "I can jump exactly twenty-nine feet, eleven inches. And if you don't believe me, ask Ratsputin."

Alexy Alexy spat out Ratsputin's name as if it might poison him if it lingered too long on his tongue.

Evangeline ran to the door and locked it. Turning back to Alexy, she realized that this was the first time she had seen him without the dance master looming over him like a black shadow. She felt she was seeing Alexy for the very first time.

"Where is he now?" she asked. "Where is Ratsputin?"

Alexy paused as if he were about to say, *Ratsputin is at this very moment selling Girl Scout cookies to the president of the United States of America.* What he actually said was, "He's taking a bath. A *bubble* bath."

Evangeline brought her hand up to her mouth to stifle the shout that wanted to escape like a canary from an open cage. To think of that horrible man sitting in a big bathtub of bubbles like a googling baby was too much. Alexy might as well have told her that the dance master played with paper dolls.

"Every morning at six o'clock and every night at nine, like clockwork," he continued. "First he takes his constitutional, then he takes his bath. He never misses them."

"First he takes his *what?*" Evangeline asked.

"His constitutional," Alexy explained. "His walk. He gets up at five and walks for thirty minutes."

"And then he takes a *bubble* bath?" Evangeline asked, just to be sure.

Alexy nodded as if to signal that mere words could not convey how preposterous the truth sometimes is, but Evangeline knew that people could be very surprising.

"Golden-haired apes are who they are, no more, no

less," her mother sometimes said. "But human beings? Well, human beings are who they are, *plus*. And it's that *plus*, darling, that sometimes tells you more about the person than all the rest of him put together."

At least, thought Evangeline, *it explains one thing. The Baby Bubbles.*

But Alexy had not jumped to the second story to talk about bubble baths.

"Ratsputin knows your real name," he said. "He knows that your real name is Evangeline Mudd!"

Evangeline felt her heart drop into her stomach. So it wasn't just a lucky guess!

"But how?" she finally managed to ask.

Alexy walked over to Evangeline's bag, which she had deposited beside her bed. He pointed to the yellow luggage tag on which Evangeline had practiced with the fountain pen.

"He read it!" she cried.

"All the while you were standing there, he was taking you in. He was watching the way you shifted your feet. He was watching the way you moved your lips when you talked. He was watching your ears and your fingernails and your eyelashes and every hair on your head."

Evangeline could feel goose bumps popping out on

her arms and legs. It gave her a terrible case of the heebie-jeebies to think that Ratsputin had been watching her so closely.

"He was reading *you* just the way he read the luggage tag," Alexy Alexy continued. "Ratsputin is a wicked man. A very wicked man."

Of this Evangeline had no doubt. She had sensed it from the moment he had opened the door at Mudd's Manor. But to hear someone actually say it, actually say out loud that another person was *wicked,* caused a shiver to run down the back of her spine.

"But why are you here with him?" she asked. "Why don't you go home to your parents?"

Almost immediately Evangeline wished she had remained silent.

"I'll never see my parents again," Alexy replied.

Evangeline was sure that she hadn't heard the boy correctly. The idea that she might never see Merriweather's dreamy, faraway smile or hear Magdalena say her name was so impossible that it nearly took the girl's breath away. It was unthinkable.

For his part, Alexy turned toward the window and looked out into the night. Evangeline thought she heard something that sounded like a sniff, but when Alexy looked up to face her again, his cheeks were dry.

"Is it because of Ratsputin?" she finally managed to ask. "Is it because of *him* that you'll never see your parents again?"

Alexy nodded just once as he looked directly into Evangeline's eyes. It seemed to the girl that all the sadness that ever was, and all the sadness that ever had been, and all the sadness that ever would be had come together at just that moment to find a home in Alexy Alexy.

Chapter 15

Skrunchklôkker

T he boy took a step toward the window, and for a moment, Evangeline wondered if he was going to leave.

I've got to say something, she told herself, *something to give him hope.*

But before she thought what it was that she might say, Alexy turned back toward her.

"I was born in Macaronia," he said.

Evangeline thought she had heard of Macaronia, but she couldn't quite place it on the map.

"My parents had a tiny farm. We grew beet."

"Don't you mean beets?" Evangeline asked.

"No," Alexy responded. "Beet. We were so poor and

our farm was so tiny that we grew just one beet a year."

Yikes! Evangeline thought. *That* is *poor!*

"But we were very happy," the boy said, as if he suspected what Evangeline had been thinking. "I had my parents, and they had me. Even as a toddler, I could jump. My father used to tease me and tell me that I was part kangaroo. People used to come from all the other villages just to watch me. It was just something I could do. It was fun."

Evangeline thought of all the happy hours she had spent brachiating in the trees that surrounded the cozy bungalow in New England.

"But all that changed on my fourth birthday," Alexy continued. "I woke up with a dangerous fever. My parents didn't have the money to send for a doctor, but my mother knew of a plant that could cure the cough that was racking my body. We call it *überpeepn, überpeepn sa torta.*"

"*Über*-what?" asked Evangeline. It sounded like an awfully complicated name for just a plant.

"Eyebrow of the turtle," Alexy explained. "My mother knew of only one place where it thrived—our neighbor's garden."

From the way Alexy said the word *neighbor,* as if he almost couldn't bear to form the word, Evangeline didn't have to guess who that neighbor was.

"Ratsputin!" she said.

"Ratsputin," the boy repeated. "My father begged him to give us just one sprig of the *überpeepn,* just one, but he wouldn't."

"What a creep!" Evangeline said.

She knew it wasn't nice to call people names, but she couldn't help it. Ratsputin really was a creep.

"Finally, on a night when I lay on my bed burning with fever, my father stole into Ratsputin's garden and plucked an *überpeepn* leaf. It wasn't right, but what else could he have done?"

Alexy looked directly at Evangeline, as if he expected an answer.

"Nothing," she said. "There was nothing else he could have done. I would have done the same thing."

"The minute my father had the leaf between his fingers, Ratsputin came tearing out of his house. 'Thief!' he cried. 'Thief!' The leaf my father had taken was no bigger than a blade of grass, but it was too late. He had stolen it, and Ratsputin had caught him."

"But your father was saving your life," Evangeline said. "Couldn't he explain to the police why he had done it?"

"The chief of police is Ratsputin's brother, and just as wicked. Ratsputin knew he had my father. If he reported him for stealing, my father would have been sent away to a *skrunchklôkker*."

Evangeline didn't know what a *skrunchklôkker* was, and she didn't want to know.

"My parents begged for mercy. Ratsputin finally told them that there was only one condition that would make him not report my father."

"What?" asked Evangeline. The boy's story had her sitting on the very edge of the bed. "What condition was that?"

"He wanted *me*!" Alexy said.

This news was too much for the girl.

"You!" she cried much louder than she had meant to.

"Ratsputin was training dancers even then, but he wasn't doing well. His methods were too strict. He had been watching me through a secret hole he had drilled in the wall that separated our gardens. He knew that he could train me to become a dancer, a dancer that would make him very rich.

"In the end, my parents had to agree. If my father went to the *skrunchklôkker,* he would never return. My mother and I would have starved."

"And I'll bet even if your father had gone to that . . .

that . . . *skrunchklôkker,*" Evangeline said, "Ratsputin wouldn't have given your mother the *überpeepn.*"

Evangeline couldn't help but feel a little proud of how quickly she was taking to Alexy's language.

"Right," said Alexy Alexy. "They had to do it, don't you see? They had to do it to save my life."

Evangeline found herself thinking about Merriweather and Magdalena. *What would they have done?* she wondered. *Would they have given me to Ratsputin to save my life?*

"Ever since that terrible day," Alexy continued, "Ratsputin has made me train. I tried to run away once, but before I was out the door, Ratsputin was on the phone to his brother. And when I came back, he doubled my training. Even now, it's always, 'Higher, Alexy! Higher! More, Alexy! More!' "

Alexy had told his entire story rooted to one spot, as if he would have been unable to finish had he moved. But now, it seemed, he had said everything he intended to. He turned back toward the window.

But there was still one thing that Evangeline didn't understand.

"But why did Ratsputin do it in the first place?" she asked. "Why did he want you?"

"Why do you think?" Alexy asked right back.

"Money! People pay a great deal of money to see me dance. Ratsputin keeps it all. Ratsputin is a very, very rich man, and with every jump, I make him richer."

"But that's *your* money," Evangeline said. "You are the one dancing. You are the one practicing day after day."

"I've never seen a cent," Alexy answered. "And my parents are just as poor as they ever were."

"It should be the *skrunchklôkker* for Ratsputin," said Evangeline.

"Things don't always turn out the way they *should*," Alexy said bitterly.

Evangeline knew that what Alexy Alexy had said was true. Things didn't always turn out the way they should, but she also knew that sometimes they did.

After all, she reasoned, *look what happened to me. It looked like my parents had disappeared in the Ikkinasti Jungle. It looked like I had lost them forever, just the way it looks like Alexy Alexy has lost his. But I didn't, and even though it was hard to go to Ikkinasti, the hardest thing I have ever done, it was worth it, because in the end, things* did *turn out.*

Evangeline stood up.

"We'll make them," she said.

Alexy stopped.

"Make them?" he said.

"We'll make things turn out the way they should," the girl said.

Even though she was speaking softly, her voice was strong and full of confidence. Now Alexy was looking at *her* as if he were seeing her for the first time.

Evangeline could feel her face turning red. She wasn't used to being looked at so closely, especially by a boy.

"I've done it once," she said. "Maybe I can do it again."

Alexy continued to look.

"Who are you, anyway?" he finally asked.

Alexy listened to Evangeline's story just as he had told his own, without moving a muscle.

"The trouble is," she ended, "Melvin is keeping the location of the mink ranch top secret. I don't know where it is."

What Alexy said next caused Evangeline to sit back down on the bed.

"But I do," he whispered. "I know exactly where it is."

Chapter 16

*Tree... wrong...
direction... I.T. ...*

Silence fell over the room as Evangeline pondered what Alexy had told her. He might as well have pulled a rhinoceros from under her bed.

Since I have arrived at Mudd's Manor, my only goal has been to discover where Melvin's ranch is, and all along, the only thing I had to do was ask Alexy. Sometimes, she decided, *life is very nearly like a gigantic puzzle. All the pieces you need are right there on the table, even the ones that you think are missing.*

For his part, Alexy couldn't take his eyes off Evangeline. In all his traveling around the world, dancing for kings and queens and sheiks and maharajahs and maharanis, he had never met anyone like her.

Evangeline turned toward the window.

"I've got to get to that mink farm," she said.

"Why didn't you say so?" Alexy asked. "Dancers have good memories for that kind of thing. We have to, or we'd find ourselves in the orchestra pit."

Evangeline hadn't thought about it before, but, yes, what Alexy Alexy said made sense. After all, dancers are always turning this way and that, going here and there and then whirling around and prancing back in the way they had just come from. If a dancer didn't have a good sense of direction, he could end up in a terrible mess.

Evangeline tuned back to face the boy. He closed his eyes, and she could see the fine lines that were forming across his forehead as he concentrated.

"First," he began, "we—"

"Wait!" Evangeline interrupted.

She ran to her bag to get her fountain pen and a sheet of paper.

"Okay," she said, once she had screwed the cap off the pen and settled down on the bed. "Go ahead."

"Okay, then . . ." Alexy began again. "First we drove straight through town . . . four . . . no . . . five blocks."

Straight through town, Evangeline wrote, *4 . . .* She scratched that out with an *X* as Alexy corrected himself,

101

but in her excitement she'd pressed too hard on the nib. A stream of ink squirted out across the page and onto the tip of her index finger. *5 blocks,* she wrote.

"We turned left at a grocery," Alexy continued. "A produce truck was unloading beets. It reminded me of home."

Turn left . . . grocery . . . beets. The words appeared on the paper like parts of a secret code.

"Then there was a big tree. All its limbs were growing in the wrong direction. It looked like India Terpsichore covered with bark."

Tree . . . wrong . . . direction . . . I.T.

"And then we went up a long hill. It seemed like it took forever to get to the top, and when we did, we passed a tulip farm. Aunt Tillie's Tulips or something like that. Some workmen were building a wall around it . . . and then . . . and then . . ."

Alexy opened his eyes. Evangeline lifted her pen from the paper.

"It's no good," he said. "It gets too complicated. I could *take* you. It's just that I can't *tell* you. It's more like I can *feel* the way there."

Evangeline understood this perfectly. She had once tried to explain to someone how to brachiate, but the minute she tried to put it into words, she realized how wrong it all was. Someone trying to brachiate by following her directions would probably end up on the ground.

Alexy looked over at the clock on the dresser. Nine twenty.

"I've got to go," he nearly shouted. "If Ratsputin finds out I'm not in my room, he'll—"

But Evangeline never learned what horrible punishment the dance master would inflict on Alexy because at that exact moment, one of the floorboards in the manor's magnificent upstairs hallway creaked.

Both Evangeline and Alexy froze. Evangeline brought her finger to her lips, crept over to the door, and put her ear to the keyhole.

Was it her imagination or could she actually hear the rise and fall of someone's breathing? And then, as if to say, *No, it's not your imagination. It's absolutely real!* the unmistakable scent of Baby Bubbles came wafting through the keyhole. There could be no doubt about it; the dance master was on the other side.

Evangeline could feel the hairs on the back of her neck come to attention as she pointed to the door. Alexy didn't need to be told twice. He backed toward the window, and before Evangeline realized what had happened, he hopped through it, out into the night.

I hope he can jump down as well as he can jump up, Evangeline thought. At the same time, it came to her that even if Alexy made it to the ground, the danger wasn't over. He needed time to get back in his room.

In the jungle, it's the master of surprise who survives, she could almost hear her father saying.

Without knowing what the outcome might be, Evangeline yanked back the lock and pulled the door open. The dance master, dressed in black silk pajamas and a robe to match, fell like a domino, flat across the threshold.

"Excuse me, Miss Libby Rick," he muttered, after he stood up. "I was tying my shoe. I must have lost my balance."

The way he said *Rick* with such a hard *K* and practically rolling the *R* almost made it seem like he was spitting at her.

"That must have been difficult," Evangeline said, glancing down at his feet. "Since you're not wearing shoes, I mean."

But Ratsputin was not about to be caught off balance twice in one night by the girl.

"I see that your window is open," he said, raising an eyebrow.

The way he was concentrating on the window reminded Evangeline of one of those fancy machines that doctors use to look right through you. She took a step toward the window, partially to distract Ratsputin's

gaze and partially to stop the trembling in her knees.

"I like fresh air," she said, shrugging and spreading her hands out in front of her.

Ratsputin smiled in a way that made Evangeline think of a snake stretching itself on a blistering rock.

"It's a dangerous practice," he hissed, slithering into the hallway. "You never know what might jump in."

Chapter 17

Pink... Ratsputin...
Pink... Ratsputin...
Pink... Ratsputin...

Evangeline turned the lock, its sharp click bringing her back to herself and helping to erase the image of Ratsputin's smile, which seemed to hang in the air like a kite. It was then that she noticed the pink stain on her fingertip. To her own amazement, she discovered that she could not stop looking at that pink inkblot. She couldn't get over the crazy feeling that it was trying to tell her something and that, whatever it was, it was somehow connected to Ratsputin and that if she could only figure it out, it would solve a big problem.

Pink . . . she thought . . . *Ratsputin . . . Ratsputin . . . pink . . .*

She could feel the two words going round and round. They were like those crazy wrestlers that you see on television, circling each other but not daring to get close.

Pink . . . Ratsputin . . . pink . . . Ratsputin . . . pink . . . Ratsputin . . .

What is it? she asked herself over and over again. *What is it?*

And then Evangeline caught the tiniest whiff of Baby Bubbles, its scent still wafting around the room. Suddenly *pink* and *Ratsputin* and *Baby Bubbles* came together like long-lost relatives at an airport. And just as when two relatives come together they form a family, when *pink* and *Ratsputin* and *Baby Bubbles* came together, they formed an idea, an idea so bold that Evangeline nearly shouted.

Of course! she thought. *That's it!*

If the room had been hung with trapezes, she would have brachiated in pure joy.

The idea required some risk, of course, like almost all good ideas. But Evangeline was the kind of girl who was used to taking risks. Going to the Ikkinasti Jungle had required risk. Coming back to Mudd's Manor to save the minks required risk. Telling everybody that her name was Libby Rick and that she was from the Ballerina Hall of Fame required risk. In fact, it seemed to Evangeline that almost anything worth doing required taking a risk.

"It's so simple," she told herself as she turned down the sheets. "It's so simple."

She put on her pajamas, set her alarm clock, and hopped into bed. But at five o'clock the next morning, she was fully dressed and standing with her ear against her bedroom door. Just as she had hoped, at a minute or two after five, she heard the hall floorboard creak.

That's him, she thought. *He's going for his constitutional.*

She counted to fifty to give Ratsputin time to get downstairs and out of the house. Then she counted to fifty again, just to be safe.

"Forty-eight . . . forty-nine . . . fifty!"

She opened the door the tiniest crack, listening for the muffled squeak or the hushed footstep that might indicate someone was up and about. Nothing. She pulled the door toward her until the opening was wide enough to thrust her head out into the hallway. She looked first to the left and then to the right.

"Not a soul," she whispered.

Patting the pocket of her shirt, she assured herself that what she needed for her plan to succeed was there.

"Thank you, Magdalena," she said. "Thank you, Merriweather."

She stepped out into the hallway.

Arriving at the enormous bedroom that belonged to India Terpsichore and Melvin, Evangeline put her ear to the double doors carved with hundreds of India Terpsichores cavorting around their perimeters. These carvings always reminded Evangeline of a buffalo stampede, except that instead of buffaloes, it was hundreds of India Terpsichores running like mad.

From inside the room, Evangeline could hear what sounded like the rumblings of a tremendous thunderstorm—the twin snorings of her father's second cousin, twice removed, and his wife.

Evangeline moved on until she came to the door of the room occupied by Alexy Alexy. She had already decided that the boy had made it safely back into his room. If he hadn't, there would have been a hubbub.

Moving quickly away from Alexy's door, Evangeline continued down the hall until she arrived at her destination—the last doorway, the one that led to the room of the dance master. Was it a bit chilly in the hall, or was it the thought of the dance master that caused her to shudder? Standing in front of Ratsputin's door, she could feel her resolve begin to waver.

Maybe I should go back, she thought. *I don't want to end up in a* skrunchklôkker *somewhere.*

But then she remembered something her piano teacher, Madame Valentina Kloudishkaya, had once told her.

"Do you know ze difference between a good pianist and a grrreat one?" the woman had asked.

"Technique?" Evangeline had guessed. "Strong hands? A good memory?"

"No," Madame Kloudishkaya said, waving her arms as if these were nothing more than mosquitoes buzzing around her ears. "No. Ze grrrreat pianist never doubts herself. Vunce she allows her fingers to hit ze keys, she never looks back."

Checking her pocket a final time, Evangeline put her hand on the doorknob. As quietly as a golden-haired ape walking along a jungle path, she opened Ratsputin's door and ran in.

Minutes later, she was back in her own room, panting from excitement and biting her cheeks to keep from laughing at her own daring. It had gone perfectly. The only evidence was the scent of the Baby Bubbles, which had attached itself to her hands like a pair of invisible gloves when she had unscrewed the lid.

She took the pen from her pocket. She very much would have liked to have written a note to Magdalena and Merriweather, telling them what she had done. But she knew that was impossible. The pen was completely out of ink.

Chapter 18

The SPMs

"Eeeeeeiiiiiiiiiiiiiiiioooooooooiiiiiiiiiiiiiiiiiayayayayayay!"
It was a hideous noise, worse than a thousand fingernails tearing their way across the surface of a blackboard, but to Evangeline, it was sweeter than a lullaby. She stood up on the bed and bounced so high that her curls grazed the ceiling.

"It worked!" she shouted. "It worked!"

She glanced over at the china clock: 6:05. She hopped off the bed and ran out into the hall, where she discovered Melvin, standing in the doorway of his bedroom, thrusting the air in front of him with a baseball bat. India Terpsichore was standing behind him, and across the hall, Alexy Alexy was peering out of his own doorway, yawning and scratching his head.

The CEO, still in his mink pajamas, held his fingers up to his lips.

"Animal nuts!" he whispered as he jabbed the baseball bat into the empty hall. "Animal nuts are in the house!"

His eyebrow was going crazy.

Evangeline barely recognized India Terpsichore. Her head was wrapped in a rubbery-looking thing, and her face was slathered with layers of cream.

That must have been exactly what the tyrannosaurs looked like when they were changing into buzzards, Evangeline thought, unable to take her eyes off the preposterous woman.

"As a rudely awakened ballerina who has not let herself go, I demand to know who is making that racket," croaked India Terpsichore.

Alexy Alexy said nothing but looked steadily toward Ratsputin's door, from whence the screaming seemed to have emanated.

For a moment, silence lingered in the hallway as if it were hanging around waiting for something more to happen.

"Maybe we imagined it," Melvin said at last, letting his baseball bat drop weakly to his side.

"Maybe *you* imagined it," his wife snapped, "but I

know what I heard and what I heard was—"

"Eeeeeeiiiiiiiiiiiiiiiiiooooooooooiiiiiiiiiiiiiiiiayayayayay!"

Not one second later, Ratsputin's door was thrown open, and the dance master himself catapulted into the hallway.

"Loooooooook at meeeeeeeeeeee!" he bellowed.

It was completely unnecessary for him to have made this demand, because the others couldn't help but look at him. His face and neck, his hands and his feet, even his fingernails and the insides of his ears—all of him, in fact, that wasn't covered by his black pajamas—was the color of a freshly chewed wad of cherry-flavored bubblegum.

"You're *pink*!" India Terpsichore declared. "And, I might add, a very unbecoming shade of pink."

"I'm afraid, sir," said Melvin, whose eyebrow, now that it knew that animal nuts were not prowling about, had calmed down, "that I shall have to agree with my wife in this matter. You are practically magenta!"

"Of course I'm pink, you morons," snarled Ratsputin, throwing his hands up into the air. "I'm not blind!"

Evangeline wondered at how quickly Ratsputin had dropped the false manners that up to now he had displayed so earnestly every time Melvin or India Terpsichore was around.

"Every square inch of me is the color of a strawberry milk shake!" he hollered.

"You're wrong about that," said India Terpsichore with an indifferent flutter of the feather collar on her robe. "Quite wrong."

This seemed to give Ratsputin some hope.

"You mean I'm not as pink as I think I am?" he whined.

"Oh no," India Terpsichore responded. "You're much pinker. You said you were the color of a strawberry milk shake. But raspberry is more like it. Raspberry is a much brighter shade of pink than strawberry when you get right down to it."

This information caused Ratsputin to stamp his feet and turn the air blue with an astonishing display of what could only have been swearing of the most poisonous kind. Fortunately, however, he was speaking in Macaronian, so no one there could understand a word he was saying, except, of course, Alexy Alexy.

For his part, the boy remained silent. He seemed absolutely thunderstruck to see the man who had caused him so much misery behaving so outrageously. Occasionally, Alexy would steal a glimpse at Evangeline. But though she wanted to return his furtive glances, she steadfastly refused to even so much as blink in Alexy's direction. Instead, she clucked her tongue and shook her head.

"Who's making chicken noises?" Ratsputin shrieked.

"I'm sorry," Evangeline said, trying to sound sincere. "It's just that . . . well, it's just that—"

"It's just that what?" Ratsputin shouted. "It's just that you're a lying little sneak who is about to get what's coming to her? Is that what you were about to say?"

Evangeline hoped that this remark would not register too heavily with Melvin or India Terpsichore, which, from the way they were continuing to stare at Ratsputin, as if he were turning into a giant cone of cotton candy right before their eyes, it didn't seem to.

"I don't know how to say this," Evangeline continued just as she had rehearsed. "But, well, it looks as if you have a serious case . . . of the Screeming Pink Meemies!"

This seemed to shock India Terpsichore out of her stupor.

"The what?" she shouted.

"The Screaming Pink Meemies," Evangeline continued. "No one knows what causes them. I once knew a boy who had the SPMs. He waited too long to see a doctor, and today he is—"

"Don't tell me!" shouted Ratsputin hysterically. "He's still pink!"

"Not exactly," Evangeline said mysteriously. "He's *striped*."

"Striped?" Ratsputin's voice went up so high that he sounded like a six-year-old girl.

"Unfortunately, yes," Evangeline said in what she imagined was a clinical tone of voice. "The pink eventually fades, but not all of it. It disappears in bands, but between the bands, where it doesn't fade, it becomes permanent."

"Per-permanent?" Ratsputin stammered.

"I'm afraid so," Evangeline improvised. "Today that man looks like a human zebra, except of course he's pink and white rather than—"

Ratsputin charged at Melvin, who jumped backward as if he wanted nothing to do with anyone who was the color of stomach medicine.

But he was too late. Ratsputin had him by the very hairs of his mink collar.

"Get me to a hospital!" the dance master shouted. "NOW!"

"Yes, of course," Melvin mumbled. "Just let me change into my—"

"Nitwit!" hollered Ratsputin. "Didn't you hear what she said? There's no time for changing! There's no time for anything! We're going to a hospital, and we're going RIGHT NOW! I don't intend to look like a candy cane the rest of my life!"

Without another word, he dragged Melvin down the hall toward the steps.

"Oh, there is one other thing about the SPMs," Evangeline said quietly, glancing toward India Terpsichore.

"What's that?" the ballerina demanded.

"They're highly contagious." Evangeline paused for a moment to let this news sink in. "Especially," she continued, "to those who haven't let themselves go."

India Terpsichore leaped past Evangeline like a gazelle with its tail on fire.

"Melvinnnnnnnnnnnn!" she screamed. "Wait for meeeeeeeeeeeeeee!"

Chapter 19

It's Kind of
Like Brachiating

In a matter of seconds, Ratsputin, Melvin, and India Terpsichore had tumbled down the stairs and were racing each other to the front door.

As soon as Evangeline heard the tires of Melvin's big black car screeching out of the driveway and onto the street, she turned to Alexy Alexy. The boy was still standing, dumbstruck it seemed, in his doorway.

"Let's go," Evangeline said to the boy.

"Go?" Alexy repeated.

"To the mink ranch," Evangeline replied. "You can do it, can't you? You said you could."

"Of course I can," Alexy responded. "But what about the Screeming Pink Meemies, or whatever they are?"

"Don't worry about that," said Evangeline, moving toward her room. "Right now, we've got to get dressed. I'll explain all about it on the way."

Alexy said nothing for a moment but stared in exactly the way that had made her blush the night before.

"You . . . you mean it was *you*?" Alexy asked.

"Who else?" Evangeline replied with a smile so big and so genuine that Alexy himself broke out in one that matched hers exactly.

Evangeline realized that this was almost the first time she had ever seen her new friend smile.

"By the way," she said, looking back over her shoulder. "Did you know that Ratsputin has a rubber ducky?"

Within minutes, both Alexy and Evangeline were back in the hallway, dressed and ready to set out for Melvin Mudd's Marvelous Minks.

"But how are we going to get there?" Alexy asked as they headed toward the stairs. "It's too far to walk, especially if we have to be back before Ratsputin and the others return."

"I've been thinking about that," Evangeline replied. "Can you ride a bike?"

Alexy nodded.

"Good!" Evangeline replied. "Wait for me out front."

"What have I got to lose?" Alexy said aloud as he

opened the front door and stepped out onto the porch. "At least I won't have to spend the entire day jumping."

He had just picked up a pebble and was about to throw it toward the street when Evangeline came from around the corner of the house.

"You said *bicycle*," Alexy said, dropping the pebble.

Alexy pointed to the two unicycles that Evangeline was pushing out in front of her, one in each hand.

"I know," Evangeline replied optimistically. "But if you put these together, we would have a bicycle. Almost, that is."

"Yes, well, if you put two eggs together you have scrambled eggs," Alexy replied, taking one of the unicycles by the seat.

Now, I don't know if you've ever tried to ride a unicycle—probably not, unless you're one of those lucky kids who goes to clown camp—but take my word for it, it isn't easy. And the funny thing is, it's because unicycles are so good-natured. That is, they are always nodding, as if to say, "Yes, you are right. I agree with you completely." Unfortunately, when they nod, they tip you right off.

It did not take long, however, for Alexy Alexy to get the hang of it. He was a dancer, and dancers have an almost perfect sense of balance. In a matter of minutes, he was wheeling up and down the sidewalk, both forward and backward. He was even making the uni-cycle twirl on its one wheel.

"Hey!" he shouted. "This is fun!"

Evangeline, on the other hand, wasn't having so much fun. The second she thought she was settled in the unicycle's seat, it nodded her off.

"Something must be wrong with mine," she said, frowning. "I can't get it to work."

"All you have to do," Alexy said as he pedaled up to her, "is imagine that you are hanging from a string attached to the top of your head."

"Like a puppet, you mean?" Evangeline asked.

"Yes," Alexy answered. He backpedaled a bit to keep his balance. "Exactly like a puppet."

Evangeline closed her eyes and saw herself as a gigantic, life-size marionette. At first, this seemed impossible, even with the girl's considerable powers of imagination. But then she began to imagine her beloved mother as the puppeteer, the

124

one holding the string tight so that she couldn't fall. She opened her eyes.

"Okay," she said, climbing back onto the unicycle's seat. "Here goes." In her mind's eye, she could see Magdalena somewhere high above her, supporting her with the cross-sticks of an Evangeline marionette. Keeping her head and shoulders straight, she slowly began to work the pedals.

She traveled about five feet before she fell, but that was five feet farther than she had pedaled previously.

"Hey!" she shouted. "I almost had it!"

"I told you," said Alexy, encouraging her with his smile. "It's not that hard."

On her second try, Evangeline made it twice as far, and by the third, she was nearly as confident as Alexy himself.

"It's kind of like brachiating," she said as she zipped past him down the sidewalk.

"Like what?" Alexy asked. After all, his parents weren't primatologists. He'd never heard of the word.

But there was no time for definitions.

"I'll explain it on the way," the girl said. "Let's go!"

"Right!" Alexy replied. "Follow me!"

He zipped by Evangeline and turned right onto the sidewalk that ran parallel to the street.

Evangeline was right behind him.

Chapter 20

Gotcha!

Down the street they pedaled. The boy seemed to have no hesitation about the way to the mink farm, and as he turned left onto one street or right onto another, not once did he ever stop to think or question himself. Nor did he ever look back to see if Evangeline was behind him. He was like a honeybee headed straight for the hive.

It was still early in the morning, so there was very little traffic and even fewer pedestrians. But those who were out stopped to gawk at the two children as they raced along.

"Has a circus come to town?" a man yelled from his car window.

"Hey!" shouted another. "Don't look now, but you're missing the back wheel! Ha! Ha!"

Evangeline paid no attention whatever to these remarks, but Alexy, without slowing down or losing his balance, responded by showing off a trick or two. One time he stood up, crossed his arms, and pedaled backward. Another time, he twirled the unicycle three times in quick succession, like a human gyroscope.

Though Alexy only performed these stunts when a driver yelled something from the window, Evangeline was struck with the thought that he was doing these tricks for her too. And this caused her to blush just as she had done on those occasions when she had discovered Alexy staring at her so intently.

Evangeline guessed that about ten minutes had passed when they approached a grocery store that had not yet opened for business but in whose window a hand-lettered sign proclaimed FRESH VEGETABLES in bright red letters.

"Beets!" Alexy shouted, pointing at the store and turning his head a little so that Evangeline could hear him.

The girl understood exactly what it was that Alexy was trying to tell her. This was the grocery store where he had seen the man unloading the beets. To confirm this, Alexy made a signal with his hand and then nimbly turned the unicycle in that direction.

Without missing a stroke of the pedals, Evangeline turned right behind him.

On and on they rode. Soon the businesses and residential areas of the town began to give way to the countryside. The sidewalk ended, and the two cyclists found themselves wheeling down a little-used country road.

They were just passing by a herd of cows when Alexy raised his right hand and pointed to a tree on the banks of a stream that crossed under the road through a culvert. This tree could only be the one that had reminded Alexy of India Terpsichore.

From its trunk grew four main branches. The bottom two, which grew low to the ground, were like legs kicking out from the side in an outlandish jumping movement. The top two splayed out like arms stretching in opposite directions. Altogether, the tree looked as if it had just been pinched and were jumping right out of its roots.

It really does look like India Terpsichore, Evangeline thought as she passed the tree. *Except the tree is somehow more graceful.*

The day was beginning to warm up now, and Evangeline could feel the perspiration trickling down her back. For his part, Alexy seemed tireless as they rolled along. His legs, strong from hours spent in the

practice room, were working the pedals just as forcefully as they had when the two had first begun.

Evangeline's legs were beginning to ache a little, but she would not allow herself to think about it, knowing that if she began to concentrate on how tired her legs were, it would make them seem twice as tired as they really were. Instead, she did what she could to take in the sights around her.

Now the two started the ascent of a hill. It was one of those tricky hills too, with lots of smaller hills on the way up so that just when you think you've reached the top, you realize that, in fact, you've just started.

Evangeline was a little more than halfway up when a flowery scent began to fill the air, a scent that was becoming stronger with each revolution of the wheel on her unicycle. Ahead of her, Alexy was pointing to the left. Across a field of wildflowers, Evangeline saw that a group of workmen were taking down a scaffolding around a high cement wall that circled an area that might have been as big as a football field. Oddly, the workmen were wearing gas masks.

On the wall, someone had painted AUNT TILLIE'S TULIPS! PRIVATE! KEEP OUT!

Aunt Tillie must be incredibly selfish, the girl thought. *She doesn't even want people to see her tulips when they are blooming.*

This seemed unforgivably stingy of the woman. Evangeline had seen pictures of tulips growing on farms in Holland, and just now the bold stripes of red and pink and yellow would have refreshed the girl and renewed her energy for the task at hand.

Evangeline knew that the tulips had to be in bloom because by now their scent was so heavy in the air that it was almost impossible to breathe. It was like riding through a mist of heavy perfume.

No wonder those workmen are wearing gas masks, she thought.

The smell of the flowers was practically stinging her eyes. She was afraid that she was going to have to stop, but as she reached the top of the hill and passed Aunt Tillie's, the air began to freshen again, and she was able to get her breath.

"Those are just about the strongest-smelling tulips I've ever seen," she shouted up to Alexy. "I mean *not* seen."

But Alexy hadn't heard her because of the *beat-beat-beat* of the rotors of a black helicopter approaching Aunt Tillie's from the opposite direction in which the children were riding. Evangeline watched as it circled over the tulip farm like a great black hornet and then whirred away, as if it needed to get back to the nest.

By now, Alexy had gained some distance on the girl, and as Evangeline worked to catch up, she continued to think about the tulips. There was something about them that was nagging her, as if her brain had gotten a mosquito bite, but eventually, the effort of riding the unicycle took over. By the time Alexy turned left onto a smaller road, she had completely forgotten about them.

For the next fifteen minutes or so, the route seemed incredibly complicated. Alexy was turning right and left and backtracking and, it seemed to Evangeline, going around in circles. But eventually, the boy stopped in front of a rutted path that veered off from the main road and circled around to the right through some pine trees.

"This is it!" he whispered. "Melvin Mudd's mink ranch is around that curve."

Evangeline's heart, which was already beating from the exertion of pedaling the unicycle, sped up so quickly that for a moment it felt to the girl that it was going to thump its way right out of her chest.

"We made it!" she said to Alexy. "We made it!"

Alexy said nothing, but he nodded one time.

"We'd better hide our unicycles," she said.

Alexy agreed by rolling his to the side of the road and shoving it under some bushes. Evangeline did the same.

"Let's walk through the trees," she said, "in case anyone is there."

The two began to make their way through the pines. As they walked, the pine needles crunching quietly under their feet, a powerful smell once again reached Evangeline's nose. But this was not the smell of flowers. It was a horrible smell.

Alexy was already holding his nose.

"It's the minks," he said.

Evangeline followed Alexy's lead and pinched her nose closed with her thumb and index finger.

"I'm glad I don't live next to a mink farm," she whispered to Alexy.

"What are we going to do when we actually get there?" Alexy asked.

But Evangeline, realizing that she really didn't have a plan, pretended not to hear him.

One thing at a time, she thought. *I'll think of something.*

Suddenly the trees left off, and Evangeline and Alexy found themselves in a cleared area around which there was a barbed-wire fence. In front of the fence, a sign was posted.

MELVIN MUDD'S MARVELOUS MINKS
Melvin Mudd, chief executive officer

PRIVATE! NO TRESPASSING!
ANIMAL NUTS, THIS MEANS YOU!

"Look!" Alexy said, holding his nose with one hand and pointing to the gate behind the sign with the other. "There's a note taped onto the gate."

But it wasn't the note that had caught the girl's attention. The gate was swinging on its hinges, creaking in the breeze. Through the gate Evangeline could see the cages that held the minks, but like the gate, the doors to all the cages stood open. The cages were empty!

Evangeline ran to the gate and tore at the note.

Dear Animal Nuts, she read. *Gotcha! Ha!*

It was signed *Melvin Mudd.*

Chapter 21

Defeat

The ride back to Mudd's Manor wasn't nearly as much fun as the ride to the mink ranch. Both Alexy and Evangeline were silent, each weighted with the heavy knowledge that somewhere, possibly at that very minute, Chocolate Parfait and her strange assistant, Tweed, were turning the minks into tutus and leotards and who knows what else. Evangeline had broken her promise. *Hansel and Gretel in Kaboomistan* would be performed after all, and once again, Alexy Alexy would be forced to add to Ratsputin's riches.

As they approached Aunt Tillie's Tulips, the scent of the flowers was so overpowering that Evangeline wondered if she was going to faint. But in spite of her grief, the heavy fragrance set off a ticking at the back of her brain. It was as if a tiny alarm clock had been planted there, a clock with hands permanently stuck at the second just before the buzzer would sound.

What is it? the girl asked herself. *What is it about those tulips?*

Apparently, whoever was in the helicopter had similar questions, for Evangeline saw that the great black machine was back, hovering over Aunt Tillie's like a wasp and causing the wildflowers in the surrounding field to flatten themselves against the ground as if they were trying to hide from the great monster in the air. Eventually, however, the helicopter zoomed off in the same direction as before.

As Evangeline watched it disappear, her misery returned. To have given Alexy hope and then not to have delivered on that hope was practically more than Evangeline could bear, especially when she recalled the expression in Alexy's eyes as they discovered that the minks were gone.

It had taken her a few minutes to know what that expression meant. It wasn't sadness, exactly, though certainly there was some sadness in it; it wasn't anger, either, though anger was one of the ingredients. Finally, as they had walked silently back to their unicycles, Evangeline had understood. It was *defeat*. And not just the kind of defeat that you might feel after losing an important game or getting a bad grade on a quiz that you had really studied for. That kind of defeat happens to everybody. It was not even the defeat at having been unable to save the minks. After all, Evangeline herself had suffered that defeat. But as painful as that was to the girl, underneath, at the very bottom of her heart, she knew that she would be going back to the welcoming arms of her beloved parents.

That wasn't the case with Alexy. No, his was a larger kind of defeat; it was a bully that snickered and pointed and shouted "Loser!" at the top of its lungs.

Evangeline wrinkled her nose and sniffed, working to hold back the tears that were forming in the corners of her eyes.

Alexy had let her take the lead on the way home, but at the grocery, he finally pedaled up to Evangeline.

"It's not your fault," he said as they turned onto the sidewalk. "You did everything you could."

"But that wasn't good enough," Evangeline replied, looking straight ahead. "And now the minks are gone."

"But you tried your best," Alexy said.

Evangeline stopped pedaling and put both feet on the ground so that Alexy was forced to backpedal and do the same.

"Don't you understand?" she asked, now looking directly at the boy. "I made a promise, and I broke it. I said that I would rescue those minks, and I didn't do it. I told you we could change things, and we can't."

"It's okay," Alexy said, so softly that Evangeline had to lean forward to hear him. "I didn't really expect that we would."

There was nothing more to say. Both children resumed pedaling. Neither spoke on the rest of the ride home.

But just before they arrived at Mudd's Manor, Alexy did try to cheer up the girl by bouncing in one spot on his unicycle. It was amazing that he could cause the unicycle to jump up in the air like a pogo stick and land without so much as a bobble to one side or the other. Evangeline's sadness was too great to be soothed by such antics, but she couldn't stop herself from taking notice.

When the two walked through the front door of Mudd's Manor a few minutes later, they discovered that the place was once again thronging with dancers and musicians who, by now, were awake and rummaging through the house looking for some breakfast. Fortunately, the unicyclists were still sleeping and didn't even know that their transportation had been borrowed. Melvin, India Terpsichore, and Ratsputin were nowhere to be seen. Apparently, they were still at the hospital.

Evangeline and Alexy made their way through the crowd, not even bothering to say "Excuse me" when they bumped into someone, as they were bound to do.

As Evangeline climbed the steps, thoughts of her beloved parents tried to comfort her. She remembered the cozy bungalow in New England, and the flower garden where—

Evangeline stopped her ascent of the stairs so abruptly that Alexy, who was directly behind her, was forced to grab the railing to keep from crashing into her. The flower garden! That was it! The alarm clock buzzed like crazy!

Evangeline wheeled around and raced past Alexy, taking the wide steps two at a time.

"Come on!" she shouted out behind her. "Before it's too late!"

By the time Alexy had the presence of mind to ask, "Come on where?" or "Too late for what?" Evangeline had elbowed her way back through the dancers and musicians and was already out the door, pedaling her unicycle as if her very life depended on it.

Chapter 22

It All Makes Sense

As Alexy Alexy pedaled along trying to catch up with Evangeline, he decided that getting to know her was like learning a very complicated ballet. In the beginning, you never knew quite where you were or what you were supposed to do next, but there were moments when, if you just trusted your instincts and listened very carefully to the music, you began to move with it in such a way that you and the music were almost the same thing. This was one of those moments.

He pedaled faster.

"Are we going back to the mink farm?" he asked, for it seemed to him that that was exactly where they were heading.

"Not . . . mink . . . farm," Evangeline managed to blurt out between breaths.

There was more traffic now, and just as before, smart-alecky drivers would call out to the cyclists.

"Don't look now," one of them hollered, "but your bicycle broke."

"Hey!" another shouted as Evangeline and Alexy whizzed by. "Where's the fire?"

But this time Alexy didn't stop to show off by popping a wheelie or riding backward. He couldn't. Not if he wanted to keep up with Evangeline.

In what seemed like half the time it had taken them earlier that morning, they were at the grocery store. Evangeline was still going strong. She wasn't thinking about how her legs were aching or how her lungs felt like they were going to pop. She was thinking about only one thing—finding the minks before it was too late.

"Sometimes in life, you *do* get a second chance," her father had once told her, "and when you do, you had better snatch it the way a golden-hair grabs the last banana on the tree."

On and on they pedaled, until finally Evangeline reached her destination, the point in the road by the meadow where Alexy had originally pointed out Aunt Tillie's Tulips. She hopped off her unicycle, gasping for breath, almost tasting the fragrance that hung in the air like an invisible, dense fog.

"Why are we stopping here?" Alexy asked, wheeling up beside her. "It's impossible to breathe."

"But . . . that's . . . exactly . . . the . . . point," Evangeline responded.

Her own breath had started to return now, but perspiration was running down her forehead and over her nose like the tributaries of some mighty jungle river racing after a tropical downpour.

Alexy was still on his unicycle, but he was almost completely stationary, keeping his balance by subtly adjusting his posture on the seat and putting opposite pressure on each of the pedals. He reminded Evangeline of one of those characters from Greek mythology that are half boy and half goat, except that Alexy was half boy and half unicycle.

"First you say we can save the minks," he said. "Then you say it's too late. Now, here we—"

"Just tell me one thing," Evangeline interrupted. "What do you smell?"

"What do I smell?" Alexy repeated. "Tulips, of course!"

"No, you don't," Evangeline said, squinting as the perspiration found its way into the corners of her eyes. "You smell *roses*!"

Alexy tilted his head to one side and looked at Evangeline as if he were thinking that the disappointment of not finding the minks had been a bit too much for her.

"I'm not crazy," Evangeline said. "Take a whiff, a big whiff. You know what roses smell like, don't you?"

"Of course I do," Alexy replied. "Ballet dancers are always given big bouquets of them after a performance, even the boys."

"Then go on," Evangeline insisted. "Do it! I dare you!"

Alexy caused the unicycle to revolve in a circle as he began to draw in air through his nostrils. Then, with his eyes widening, he took in more and more until his lungs were filled to capacity. Evangeline could see from his expression that she was right. There was no mistaking it. It was the scent of roses that was hanging so heavily in the air.

His unicycle wobbled dangerously to the right. But in a flash, he was up on the pedals, adjusting his balance. To prove to himself, or perhaps to Evangeline, that he had not lost his balance, he flexed his knees and caused the unicycle to hop off the ground.

"But how . . ." he started to say once the unicycle had landed.

"That's what I remembered on the steps when I

started thinking about the garden at the cozy bungalow. Tulips don't have a scent! I should have known that the first time we rode by, but I was thinking so much about the minks that I guess I couldn't. And once I realized *that,* I realized that it was the smell of roses that was coming from Aunt Tillie's! And not even real roses, but some kind of cheap perfume. That's why the workmen were wearing gas masks. They wouldn't have to do that if there were real roses behind those walls."

"But I don't get it," Alexy said, finally getting a sentence out. "Aunt Tillie's is a tulip farm!"

"Is it?" Evangeline asked mysteriously. "Take another whiff, and this time concentrate on the *bottom* of the smell."

"The *bottom* of the smell?"

"Have you ever seen those really old maps of the world?" Evangeline asked.

The dance was speeding up so quickly that Alexy finally lost his step.

"I thought we were talking about roses . . . or . . . or perfume . . . or tulips."

"The really old ones." Evangeline went on as if they had been speaking of maps all along.

"You mean like the ones that show a globe resting on the back of a turtle?" Alexy asked.

"Exactly," Evangeline answered. "Now close your eyes and imagine that the globe is the scent of that perfume."

"But—" Alexy protested.

"Just do it!" Evangeline said a bit more strongly than she had meant to. "Please," she added. "We don't have much time."

Alexy did as Evangeline asked, once again drawing in air through his nostrils, imagining the ancient map as he did so. Yes. There was the cheap, acrid smell of the rose perfume—that was the globe.

"Okay," he said. "I've got it!"

"And now," she continued, nearly whispering, "imagine that there is another scent, underneath the perfume just the way the turtle is underneath the globe."

At first Alexy could smell nothing but the perfume, but then as he concentrated on the turtle, another scent began to make its presence known, faint at the beginning—so faint that he wasn't sure if it was even there—but as he continued to draw in air, the scent became clearer and clearer, and the turtle transformed itself into another animal.

"It's the minks!" he shouted, opening his eyes and releasing the tremendous breath he had just taken.

"It all makes sense," Evangeline went on. "The high wall around a tulip farm, the overpowering smell of

147

roses, even Melvin's saying that he had another trick or two up his sleeve, and then there was that stupid joke about being a *blooming* idiot. I'll bet you anything that there is no Aunt Tillie and that the minks are behind those walls. He moved them there to keep PUFF from finding the mink ranch! And to disguise the smell, he's got big vats of perfume or something."

Alexy hadn't been there to hear Melvin's joke, of course, but he had to agree with Evangeline.

"What are we waiting for?" he shouted, turning toward Aunt Tillie's. "Let's go!"

But he had not taken two steps when a cry of dismay escaped from Evangeline's lips.

"Oh no!" she shouted as she pointed to the bottom of the hill they had just ridden up. "Look!"

Alexy turned to see a figure furiously pedaling a unicycle on the road just before the steep rise of the hill. The figure was dressed entirely in black, but his face and hands were the color of ripe raspberries.

Chapter 23

Bolted on the Inside

"**R**atsputin!" Evangeline shouted.

But Alexy was already running through the field toward Aunt Tillie's. With a final glance at the figure on the unicycle, Evangeline ran after him.

The grass in the field was waist high and dotted with clumps of wildflowers—yellow goldenrod, blue cornflowers, and others too, which Evangeline didn't

know. She only noticed the flowers at all because of the number of bees that were working them. There were hundreds of them, flying in squadrons from blossom to blossom. The air vibrated around her with their buzzing.

There must be a hive around here somewhere, Evangeline thought, taking care to avoid the flowers as she ran. The idea of making so many bees angry was almost as terrifying as the sight of Ratsputin pedaling furiously on the unicycle.

To her immense relief, Evangeline followed Alexy out of the field and into the clearing that held Aunt Tillie's. The nearer she got to the newly built wall, the stronger the smell of the minks became.

"No wonder those workmen were wearing gas masks," Evangeline panted, cupping her hand over her nose and mouth.

But Alexy hadn't heard her. He had already reached the wall and had run off to the left, heading toward the corner.

"Go the other way!" he called back over his shoulder. "We've got to find the entrance."

Evangeline took off toward the right. The wall, on that side at least, was as blank as a newly erased blackboard, with neither door nor window. Occasionally, she would have to hop over sections of the scaffolding that the workmen had left behind, and once she stumbled over one of the long pipes that were scattered on the ground around the wall like a game of giant pick-up sticks. But riding the unicycle had strengthened her sense of balance, and she soon righted herself and found her stride.

When she reached the corner, she turned left, following the wall, but she discovered that this side of the wall, too, was as blank as the first. As she rounded the next corner, Evangeline saw Alexy heading toward her. She also saw that they weren't alone. A workman was standing in front of a large gray metal door that had been inset into the wall.

"Forgot my tools," he said as Evangeline ran up to him. "Always forgettin' my tools."

"Must . . . get . . . inside . . ." Evangeline panted, noticing the name *Elvis* embroidered with blue thread onto the man's white canvas overalls. She pointed to the door, which, she was dismayed to find, had neither latch nor lock.

Elvis looked at Evangeline as if she had just suggested that they turn themselves into turnips.

"Ain't nobody gettin' in there. Noooooooo-body!" he replied, picking up a red toolbox with one hand and scratching his head with the other. "Bolted on the inside!"

As Evangeline pleaded with Elvis, Alexy Alexy backed

away from the wall, studying it as intensely as if it were the Leaning Tower of Pisa. It took her only a fraction of a second to understand what Alexy was planning to do.

How high was it that Alexy said he could jump? Evangeline shut her eyes, trying hard to remember the exact number. *Yes, that was it. Twenty-nine feet, eleven inches.*

"How high is the wall?" Alexy asked Elvis.

"That there wall?" Elvis asked. "That there wall is exactly *thirty* feet high. And I oughta know because I helped build every square inch of it."

The workman walked away from the children, daintily lifting his legs over bits of the scaffolding that lay in his path.

Thirty feet! An inch higher than Alexy Alexy had ever jumped. Now, to you and me, an inch may not seem like much, but an inch can seem like a mile when you add it to 359, which is how many inches there are in twenty-nine feet, eleven inches. Besides, Alexy himself had told Evangeline that he would never be able to jump that high. It was impossible.

Evangeline looked over her shoulder, expecting at any minute to see the dance master round the corner.

"Maybe we can make some kind of ladder," she was saying, but when she looked back, Alexy was already in the air. Evangeline gasped. Alexy was like a bird.

No, Evangeline thought, *that isn't right. He is like a boy who can fly.*

One leg was straightened out behind him in a perfect line, while the other was pulled up at the knee, almost parallel to his waist. His arms were held out in a circle in front of him, but a circle opened at the hands, as if he were rushing toward the sky in order to embrace it. His neck was straight and long and proud, and his head, in profile, reminded Evangeline of museum sculptures that had been carved thousands of years ago and that had white cards in front of them that said things like "Head of a Boy."

But it was the expression on Alexy's face that caused Evangeline to marvel so. It was an expression that she had never seen on a person her own age or of any other age for that matter. At first, she wasn't sure what to call it—there didn't seem to be a word to describe it. The closest she could get wasn't even a word that Evangeline herself could ever remember using, and yet it seemed to be the only one that came close to what she was seeing.

Joy! Evangeline decided

It was joy that was shining from Alexy's eyes, and joy, too, that was radiating from his very bones and shimmering on his skin. Joy was filling the air around him with an almost visible brightness.

Watching Alexy sail through the air was the closest Evangeline had ever come to seeing human perfection. She had always wondered if there really were angels.

Now, she thought, *I know one.*

Up and up he went.

"Go, Alexy!" Evangeline called out. "Go!"

And when he lighted at last on top of the wall, as sure and as steady as a swallow might land on a cliff-side, Evangeline applauded and yelled and jumped.

"Thirty feet!" Alexy called down to her. "I did it!"

"Yes!" Evangeline answered. "Yes, you did!"

But both Alexy and Evangeline understood that there was no time for celebration; that would come later.

Alexy looked down into Aunt Tillie's.

"You were right!" he said. "The minks are here! I can see them in their cages! And there are big open tubs of something all around the edge."

"The perfume!" Evangeline called up. "It must be the perfume."

"Yes!" Alexy answered. "And . . . and . . ."

He looked down at Evangeline and rubbed his eyes as if he couldn't believe what he had seen.

"And what?" Evangeline asked.

"And a baby elephant!" he answered.

Chapter 24

Yiiiii-yiiiii-yiiiii-yiiiiiiiiii!

"That elephant is none of your business! Now get down from there before I come up and get you."

It was Ratsputin. He was still on his unicycle. Apparently, from the stalks of grass and wilting flowers that were stuck to his skin and sticking out of the spokes of the unicycle's wheel, he had ridden it through the field. Evangeline immediately saw that the ink had not faded a single shade; the dance master was still the color of a blushing rose.

As he pedaled toward the spot beneath Alexy, he made the most peculiar gestures, pumping his arms and swatting the air around him like a madman. At first, Evangeline thought he was trying to propel himself forward through such antics, but as he drew closer, she could see that a bee was zooming around his head the way gondolas on a carnival ride zoom around a center pole.

"Drat that bee!" Ratsputin muttered through his teeth.

In a single movement, he hopped off the unicycle and turned to Evangeline. The girl had to fight herself not to take a step backward, but remembering her mother's words once more, she lightly pulled her hands into fists and stood her ground.

"Well, well," the dance master sneered. "If it isn't Libby Rick, or should I say"—he wrinkled his beaky nose—"Evangeline Mudd?"

"What you *should* say," Evangeline answered, "is that you're sorry for all the pain you've caused."

"I'm only sorry that I didn't put a stop to your nonsense on the doorstep," Ratsputin replied, "but I wanted to see what you were up to."

"Why?" Evangeline asked. "So you could threaten me with the *skrunchklôkker*?"

"Oh, I see that our little Alexy has been telling you the story of how we met."

He smiled in that way that always caused a chill to roll up and down Evangeline's spine.

"You let her alone, Ratsputin," Alexy called down from his perch on the wall, "or I'll—"

"Or you'll what?" Ratsputin thundered.

Evangeline wasn't sure if the fist he was shaking was at Alexy or at the bee.

"I'll tell you what you're going to do," Ratsputin continued. "You're going to come down from that wall and get back in the practice room. If you behave yourself for the next few months, I just might find it in my heart to forget about this little incident."

"Don't believe him, Alexy," Evangeline called up to her friend. "He doesn't have a heart."

159

The dance master pointed a long, bony finger at her as if it were a wand capable of the most unspeakable magic.

"I'll deal with *you* later," he threatened, as he once again turned his attention to Alexy. "But right now, you'll have to excuse me if I attend to more pressing matters. Alexy! This is your last chance. Come down from there. Now!"

"No," Alexy replied so calmly that even Evangeline was surprised.

Alexy, of course, was too far away to see the confusion that for the tiniest fraction of a second registered on Ratsputin's face. Clearly, this was the first time the boy had defied him. But Ratsputin was not one to be caught off-guard for long.

"Okay, then," he said, narrowing his eyes and shrugging, "I'll just have to come up and get you."

This hardly seemed likely, but Evangeline watched with increasing alarm as Ratsputin began to search the ground, picking up stray pieces of the scaffolding and then letting them drop, as if each had failed some kind of test. Finally, choosing a section that was at least twice as long as he was, he seemed to find just what he was looking for.

"Did I ever tell you," he said, balancing the pole in his two hands as if he were some kind of human scale, "that in my youth, I was rather good at pole-vaulting? In fact, Alexy, I was the JPVCM—the Junior Pole-Vaulting Champion of Macaronia."

Before Evangeline could do anything to stop him, Ratsputin was running toward the wall in an ungainly lope that with each step caused his head to bob like an apple in a tub of water.

A rotten apple, she thought.

He was holding the pole with both hands and at an angle that allowed it to rest lightly on his shoulder. In spite of her horror at what was happening, Evangeline could not help but notice that the bee had returned— with two of his companions.

It must be because he's so pink, Evangeline thought, remembering the garden at the cozy bungalow and how the bees always worked the pink flowers first.

Ratsputin continued running, increasing his speed until, when he was about five feet from the wall, he jammed one end of the pole into the ground. He rose from the ground like a black rocket, his feet and legs first. At the very peak of his ascent, he let go. It seemed to Evangeline that for the slightest fraction of a second Ratsputin hovered over the ground, going neither forward nor backward, up nor down. But soon enough, the laws of physics took hold, and the dance master continued his ascent toward the wall. For its part, the pole fell noisily to the ground, shuddering as if it had fainted at being in such close contact with the dance master.

But Evangeline realized immediately that something was wrong. Whereas Alexy looked as if he had been flying when he jumped to the wall, the dance master looked as if he had been *thrown*.

Perhaps it had been too many years since Ratsputin had pole-vaulted, or perhaps he had been lying about it in the first place and had only said he was a champion to scare the children. But whatever he had said, the

truth was he was now spinning out of control, head to heels, like some kind of human Frisbee.

"Yiiiiiii!" he hollered with each revolution. "Yiiiii-yiiiii-yiiiii-yiiiiiiiiiii!"

Higher and higher he went, until finally, with one last *yiiiii,* he sailed completely over Alexy and dropped behind the wall into the mink farm as black and as heavy as a cannonball.

The next thing Evangeline heard sounded like a very large man falling into a very small pool. An instant later, the scent of cheap perfume floated down, enveloping her like an invisible veil.

"He landed in the perfume!" Alexy hollered.

"Quick!" Evangeline shouted. "Jump down and let me in."

Almost before she had finished, Alexy disappeared, and Evangeline heard all kinds of clanks coming from the other side of the door as he worked to pull back the bolts that had been shutting them out.

"One more," she heard him say.

As she waited, Evangeline put a hand to her forehead, just the way Magdalena did when she was checking to see if her beloved daughter might have a fever.

"I feel fine," she said aloud, "but what is that buzzing in my ears?"

As Alexy struggled with the last bolt, she looked up and over her shoulder to see a black dot growing larger and larger against the cloudless blue of the sky. Soon it was close enough that the buzzing it was making took on a rhythm — *thwap-thwap-thwap-thwap-thwap* — and the dot became a recognizable shape.

"Hurry! Alexy! Hurry!" Evangeline shouted. "It's that helicopter!"

Chapter 25

You're Not Me

"**Y**ou've got to hurry, Alexy!" she shouted, turning back to the wall.

"The bolt's stuck!" Alexy shouted. "I . . . I can't get . . . it!"

"It's probably Melvin in that helicopter," she shouted back, hoping that this idea would help Alexy along. "It would be just like him to be flying around in a big black helicopter."

But then an even worse thought occurred to the girl.

Maybe it's Chocolate Parfait and Tweed, here for the minks!

The thought of coming up against the terrifying giantess caused goose bumps to pop out on the girl's arms. In the meantime, the helicopter hovered over the field and then slowly began to lower itself toward the ground, as if it were nothing more than a helium balloon being pulled by a string from below.

"Hurry!" she shouted. "It's landing!"

But the voice that answered was not Alexy's.

"What are you talking about?" barked the dance master. "Have you lost your mind?"

Even through the metal of the door, Evangeline could smell the perfume.

"Alexy!" she called out. "Alexy? Are you all right?"

"Of course he's all right, ninnypants!" Ratsputin answered. "A little knock on the head never hurt anybody."

The clanking grew louder now, as Ratsputin worked the metal of the bolt against its hasp. Evangeline looked back toward the helicopter. Only a few seconds before, its rotors had been whirring around like a giant eggbeater. Now they were barely revolving over the cockpit, as if they had finally decided that enough was enough and it was naptime.

The windows were tinted black so Evangeline was unable to see who might be inside. She was expecting the door to the great machine to slide open at any second. Mysteriously, however, it remained tightly closed. Whoever was inside was not coming out. It

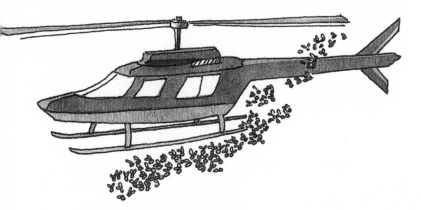

took Evangeline only a fraction of a second to understand why. She moved closer to the wall.

Thousands of angry bees were swarming the helicopter.

It must have landed on their nest, Evangeline supposed.

Evangeline was right. The helicopter *had* landed on the bees' nest, and they felt about it just the way you might feel if a helicopter landed on the roof over your room, causing all the plaster to fall down and making a huge mess that you knew *you* would be blamed for.

Communicating with each other in ways that only bees know, the black-and-yellow bombers formed themselves into a thick, wide ring that orbited the machine like one of the great rings of Saturn. Their furious buzzing was nearly as loud as the noise of the helicopter had been.

"Stop that buzzing," Ratsputin shouted at Evangeline through the door. "First you were clucking like a chicken, and now you're buzzing. Are you trying to drive me crazy?"

Before Evangeline had time to answer, the bolt gave way with a mighty clank.

"Aha!" she heard the dance master shout.

Evangeline looked over her shoulder at the bees, which had increased their numbers so that even if the windows of the helicopter hadn't been tinted, it would have been impossible to see who was inside.

"I wouldn't open that door if I were you, Ratsputin," Evangeline called out. "If you do, you might be really sorry."

She knew full well that if she told the dance master not to do something, he would almost certainly do it. Still, she thought it only fair to warn him about the bees.

"I think you mean *you'll* be really sorry," the dance master snarled, pulling the door wide open, just as Evangeline knew he would. "And anyway, you're not me," Ratsputin continued.

He pulled himself up to his full height, but it was no use. He looked nothing like the frightening man she had seen on the doorstep a few days ago. The black hat, now drenched with perfume, clung to his head like a fresh crop of mold. His mustache, soaking with the stuff, looked like it might slide right off his pink lip and land on his shoes. If he hadn't been so horrid, Evangeline might have even felt sorry for him.

Alexy Alexy stood behind him, rubbing his head, and behind Alexy, Evangeline could see the minks, who began to chatter and squeal at the commotion.

"In fact, you're not even *you*," the dance master went on. "At least, you're not the you you went around telling everybody you were, and just as soon as I get into some dry clothes, you're going to get what's coming to you." He turned to Alexy. "And that goes for you too!"

Ratsputin had now stepped out beyond the door. Evangeline thought she could almost see the clouds of perfume wafting toward the bees.

"What's that infernal buzzing?" Ratsputin demanded. "And what's that—" The dance master stopped mid-sentence, looking toward the helicopter just as the first molecule of perfume-laden air hit the bees.

"Helicopt-helicop—" he stuttered, trying to finish his sentence. "Helicoohooooooooooooooooo nooooo!"

In a great *S*, the bees slowly curled away from the helicopter and began zooming toward the dance master. Ratsputin stared at the bees as if he simply could not believe what he was seeing. Bright pink and smelling like the world's largest rosebush, he might as well have been a bee magnet. But then, coming to, he jerked up his knee so high that it almost touched his nose, and he whizzed past Evangeline like a marble from a slingshot.

Fast as he was, it was no use. The bees were in a pink and perfumed frenzy, and the faster Ratsputin ran, the faster they flew. He was like the Pied Piper of Hamelin, except instead of rats following him, it was bees.

"I'll get you for this, Evangeline Muuuuuuuuuuuud!" she heard him holler over the buzzing as he ran through the field. "I'll get you if it's the last thing I dooooooooo!"

The last Alexy and Evangeline saw of him, he was running toward the tree that looked like India Terpsichore. The bees were right behind him, in a thick, black, swirling line, and with every step Ratsputin took, they gained ground.

Chapter 26

Just Like the Minks

With Ratsputin running over the hill and the bees flying after Ratsputin, Evangeline knew that her chance to free the minks had finally arrived. But she also knew that whoever was in the helicopter was now free to get out. There wasn't a second to lose.

She ran through the door of the mink farm, ready to unlatch the first cage she came to. But once fully inside, she stopped in confusion at what lay before her. Cages! Rusty and filthy and lined up in rows that ran the length of the walls that surrounded them. There were hundreds of them, maybe even thousands! Each cage held a family of minks—not just a mother, a father, and a baby or two, but aunts and uncles, and grandparents, and cousins, and nieces and nephews, all jammed in together.

Some of them were hissing, baring their pointed teeth at every other mink who dared come near. Others huddled in the corners of the cages, rolled into balls, as if they thought that by behaving so, they might become invisible. Still others seemed to have given up all chance of happiness and looked out of the cages with blank, hopeless stares, while the others stole their food and ran over them as if they were nothing more than toys thrown away by a careless child.

Evangeline had thought she knew what she would find at the mink farm, but now, face to face with the actual suffering of the animals, she felt the breath leave her body in one big *whoosh*. For the first time in her life, she thought it possible that her knees might not hold her up.

I shouldn't have come here, she thought. *I should have stayed home with Merriweather and Magdalena. I should have stayed at the cozy bungalow and helped get ready for my new brother or sister, having lunch in the garden and brachiating through the trees.*

"Evangeline?" Alexy whispered.

She looked over at the boy.

"Are you all right?" he asked.

For a moment, Evangeline forgot about the minks.

He . . . he looks different, she thought.

She was right. From the moment she had met Alexy on the doorstep of Mudd's Manor, the sadness in his eyes had been as much a part of him as your own nose is a part of you. But something had changed. The sadness was still there, of course—perhaps it would always be—but almost for the first time since she had met him, it wasn't the only thing that Evangeline could see. There was something else now, something shining through and softening it. Evangeline thought she knew what it was—hope—and suddenly she knew that it wasn't just that Alexy *looked* different. He *was* different.

That was all it took. In spite of the horror she felt at what Aunt Tillie's contained, she ran toward the minks.

"Quick," she said to her new friend. "Start opening the cages!"

"What about the baby elephant?" Alexy asked as he struggled with a rusted latch. "It's at the back, with one foot tied to a stake."

"One thing at a ti—"

But Evangeline was interrupted by a voice from behind her.

"We'll take care of the elephant," it said.

Evangeline's heart nearly stopped beating. It was more of a squeak, really, than a voice.

"Tweed!" Evangeline shouted.

She wheeled around to find Chocolate Parfait's peculiar assistant standing in the doorway, her hair billowing around and concealing her face, like clouds around a mountaintop.

"You might stop us before we're through, Tweed," she cried. "But at least we can free *some* of the minks."

She turned back to the cages.

"Hurry, Alexy!" she called. "Hurry!"

With every second that passed, Evangeline expected to hear the thunderous bellowing of Tweed's employer. The next voice she heard, however, wasn't Chocolate Parfait's.

"But, Evangeline dear," it said. "We don't want to stop you. We want to help you."

Evangeline turned once more to find a figure standing behind Tweed, a figure in a yellow dress!

The sight of the Pencil standing comfortably with Chocolate Parfait's assistant seemed so wrong that Evangeline felt her brain hop against the top of her head.

"But . . ." she stammered.

"Don't you recognize your old friend?" the Pencil asked.

She lifted the enormous wig from the top of Tweed's head.

"Smudge!" Evangeline shouted. "It's you!"

This seemed to confuse the Smudge mightily, who, after all, never knew the nickname that Evangeline had given her—or was it him? Even now, Evangeline wasn't quite sure. But he—or was it she?—quickly recovered.

"Yes," said the Smudge in that squeaky voice. "It's me! It was also me who shoved the letter under your door."

"I knew our disguise was too good," B. Eversharp said to the Smudge. "That's why I sent you the photo, Evangeline. It was a kind of hint. Naturally, I couldn't put into writing that our friend here had managed to get a job as that terrible costumer's assistant so that we could keep an eye on her."

"But what are you doing here?" Evangeline asked. "How did you find out about Aunt Tillie's?"

"Oh, we got lucky on that one," B. Eversharp explained. "One of the workmen tipped us off."

"His name wasn't Elvis, was it?" Alexy asked.

"Perhaps it's better not to be too specific," the Pencil replied, smiling mysteriously. "Let's just say that he's a card-carrying member of our sister organization, Animals Are People Too. And now we had better get down to business before Melvin and Chocolate Parfait discover us. First let's get the baby elephant in the helicopter so we can reunite it with its mother. Then we'll take care of the minks."

176

Even with the four of them, it was terribly difficult to convince the elephant to get into the helicopter. In the end, it was Evangeline who managed. Her experience with the golden-haired apes of the Ikkinasti Jungle had given her a special way with animals, and she soon discovered that if she spoke to it in just the right tone of voice and tickled its trunk in just the right place, it would follow her wherever she went.

The minks weren't quite as easy. It wasn't trouble with the cages; it was the minks themselves. Having lived their lives as captives, they had never experienced any kind of freedom before. And besides, to one of Melvin's minks, an open cage meant only one thing—someone was going to get turned into a jacket.

Eventually, however, they began to understand what

the Pencil, the Smudge, Alexy, and Evangeline were up to. There were times when Evangeline herself didn't know if she was laughing or crying as she watched the minks hop out of the cages and feel the earth beneath their paws for the very first time. Imagine putting on the softest, comfiest slippers after a hard day of playing and maybe you'll know what the minks were experiencing.

The four friends said little and worked hard. By the end of the afternoon, the cages were empty. Some of the minks had headed north. Some of them headed south. Some went east. Some went west.

"Wherever they go," Evangeline said to Alexy as they watched the last of the minks run into the field, "at least now they can follow their own natures."

When it came time to say goodbye to the Pencil and the Smudge, there were hugs all around.

"Thank you," the Pencil said for a final time as she took the pilot's seat in the helicopter. "You are very brave children."

But later, when Evangeline thought about it, she decided that the Pencil was wrong. She and Alexy hadn't been brave. They had simply done what they had to do. They had followed their natures. Just like the minks.

Chapter 27

The Best Adventure of All

By the time Alexy and Evangeline had unicycled back to Mudd's Manor, word had already reached Melvin Mudd that he had been undone by the animal nuts.

"I've sent everybody home!" he announced as they walked through the front door. "The dancers! The musicians! All of them!"

"I hope he hasn't sent the unicyclists home," she whispered to Alexy. "How are we going to give their unicycles back?"

But if Alexy had wanted to answer, he wouldn't have been able to, because Melvin Mudd hadn't finished.

"It's the end of Mudd's Marvelous Minks!" he declared, pacing up and down in the entryway. "They got me! They cleaned me out! But never you mind. Melvin Mudd always has Plan B. Or, in this case, Plan P."

It wasn't at all clear to Evangeline if her father's second cousin, twice removed, understood the role she had played in his defeat. If he had, it seemed to make no difference to him.

"Plan P?" she asked.

"Perfume!" He beamed. "Why not? I got tubs of the stuff at Aunt Tillie's. I bought it wholesale for next to nothing. I'll bottle it up and sell it for zillions to the same rich ladies and gentlemen who bought mink underwear. After all, rich ladies and gentlemen deserve to smell nice, just like everyone else!"

He lowered his voice now, as if he were telling a secret.

"Of course, now that the minks are gone, I've had to cancel *Hansel and Gretel in Kaboomistan,* but just between you and me and the lamppost, I never have liked ballet anyway."

Melvin's response wasn't the only surprising one.

Apparently when India Terpsichore learned that there would be no production, no mink tutus, no baby elephant to dance on, she finally let it happen. She let herself go. All at once.

Evangeline wasn't there to see it, of course, but in her imagination, there was a loud pop, and by the time the air cleared, India Terpsichore had become the big slob she and Alexy now found in front of the television, wearing a tattered bathrobe and eating chocolates by the handfuls.

"I should have done it years ago," she piped, popping a candy in her mouth with one hand and

 using the robe as a kind of napkin with the other. "Chocolate anyone?"

Once they had recovered from the shock of seeing India Terpsichore as she really was, the two children ran upstairs to Ratsputin's room. They found it there, just as they knew they would—

the huge chest of cash that Alexy had earned dancing all over the world.

"I won't take all of it," he told Evangeline, as he counted out his share. "Just what is mine. Like it or not, Ratsputin did make me the world's highest-jumping dancer."

By the time he had taken his money, Alexy was wealthy, and there was still plenty left for Ratsputin, who came staggering in that evening. His encounter with the bees had left the dance master an entirely different person. The bees' venom had acted as an antidote to the poison that for many years had been circulating through his system. The shock was so great, of course, that he became a cutup, telling corny joke after corny joke. Fortunately, the bee event also seemed to have affected his memory.

"Hello, little boy," he said when he saw Alexy Alexy. "Did you hear the one about the cannibal and the clown?"

In the end, Ratsputin went into the perfume business with Melvin. In fact, he was responsible for the perfume's name: STING.

Naturally, Evangeline was very eager to get home to the cozy bungalow. Alexy Alexy, too, was going home to Macaronia at last. He had already telephoned his parents, who were so overjoyed to hear their son's voice that they burst into tears and cried like babies, which is the exact opposite of what you expect people to do when they are very, very happy.

Still, as content as the children were to be reuniting with their parents, when the time came for the friends to say goodbye, it wasn't easy.

"I'll never forget what you did for me, Evangeline," Alexy said.

They were at the airport; Evangeline's flight was scheduled to leave at any minute.

"We did it together," she replied.

It would have been too weird to hug, and even weirder to shake hands, and so they did nothing. But as Evangeline walked down the ramp, Alexy called to her.

"Hey!" he shouted. "Look!"

Just as she had at Aunt Tillie's, Evangeline turned to see Alexy Alexy sailing through the air.

"This is for you!" he shouted to the girl. "This is for Evangeline Mudd!"

As long as Evangeline lived, which was a very, very long time, she never forgot that picture of Alexy Alexy soaring through the air like a bird, like an angel, like a boy who could fly.

When Evangeline stepped off the ramp and into the plane, she was thankful that Rick was nowhere to be seen. But who should be assigned to the seat next to hers? None other than Libby Heck.

"Hello, Libby," Evangeline muttered as she sat down, thankful that that was all she would have to say on the long flight home. But imagine her surprise when the girl replied, "Oh, you must mean my twin sister, Elizabeth. I'm Susan."

"Oh," said Evangeline, her heart lifting a bit. "Excuse me, I thou—"

"*Suki* is a nickname for *Susan*," said the girl. "I'll bet you didn't know that."

Magdalena and Merriweather were waiting for her at the airport near the cozy bungalow, and the huggings and the kissings and the nose rubbings were even more affectionate than they had been at Evangeline's departure. But the little family did not go directly home. Instead, they made a brief stop at the hospital where, to everyone's delight, Evangeline's baby brother was born.

"We've decided to let you name him," Magdalena

said, putting the bouncing fat baby into Evangeline's arms.

Before the baby could make a peep, Evangeline already had the name.

"Alexy," she said. "Alexy Alexy Mudd."

"Lovely name!" said her father, beaming at his new son. "Much better than Bean Farmer."

And so Evangeline began her first day home from Mudd's Manor as a big sister, full of love and happiness and wonder, and that, as almost everyone knows, is the best adventure of all.